A Gap in the Records

Sybylla Press, a feminist printing and publishing co-operative, was established in 1976 in Melbourne.

Published in 1985 by Sybylla Co-operative Press and Publications Ltd
© 1985 Jan McKemmish
© Cover: Sybylla Co-operative Press and Publications Ltd

No part of this work may be reproduced in any form without written permission from the publisher.

ISBN 0 908205 03 1

Printed by Sybylla Co-operative Press and Publications Ltd
3rd Floor, 247-251 Flinders Lane
Melbourne 3000 Australia

Reprinted in 1987 by Sybylla Press

Reprinted in 1992 by Harvey Printing,
1A Highett Place, Fitzroy. 3065

Typeset in Plantin by Abb-Typesetting Pty Ltd
Collingwood, Victoria

Cover illustration Sava Pinney
Graphics by Sava Pinney
Maps by Jan McKemmish
Edited by Jennifer Lord and Jan Fraser

A Gap in the Records

by

Jan McKemmish

Sybylla Co-operative Press and Publications
1985

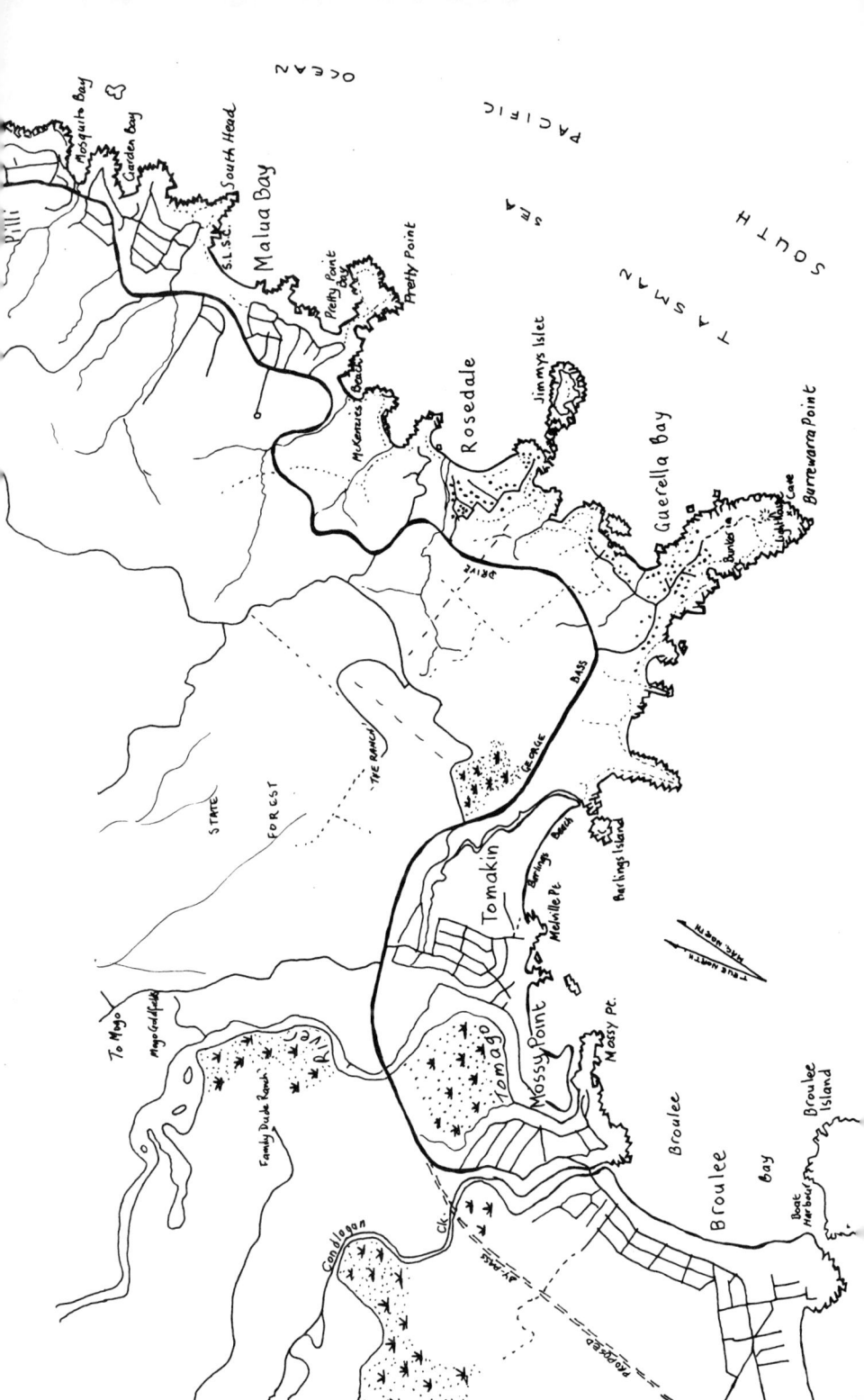

I

It's a saxophone-before-dawn time

It's a saxophone-before-dawn time.
It is blue music on a black night. No moon. No stars.
It's the moment before a story begins. A moment, just that and no more.
There is no silence.
Spiders talk in whispers.
The moment of illumination. Dawn.
A saxophone plays.
Mary Stevens appears. She is a middle-sized woman, quite plain in the grey light. She reads the letter again, folds it and puts it away in a book. Just one that is close at hand.
No.
The year is 1983.
It's a golden day at Guerella Beach. The sun is gold. White-gold. What would be the relentless Australian sun if you weren't on your Four Week Annual and it wasn't January 1980. The letter came out of the sky. It dropped in a plane at Bateman's Bay and was waiting for Cecil at the 'ranch' where he was wont to go for a martini at five. The letter found him there, serene, slightly drunk and listening to the American talk.

Joan and Amelia, drunk and still drinking, loll in chairs and laugh — the laughter that tries to conjure up courage, that is also triumphant. They drink a toast. To those who have nothing to lose. No. To success. A strong smile. Eyes that shine back. They sober. Drink strong coffee. Run through the steps again. The plan is set in motion. Many things could happen. They begin again the lists and notes that are the theorist's make-work. The night passes without their sleeping. They drink more coffee before they set off. Separate. From now on they are strangers.

Has the gun gone off on the first page? Pulp fiction conventions require it, or at least a reference to a corpse (actual or potential). I disrupt (only) a little to begin with. My first corpse isn't fiction and it is on page 2.

Susan was seventeen. She looked as the frozen image of Marilyn Monroe was supposed to. Honey-blonde, a lovely body dumb of its representation though it was rumoured she once swam naked in the local pool at night and if she did, although it was only a rumour and nasty at that, she made sure there was no moon and giggled and knew the embarrassment of local boys who rarely spoke to women, preferred to move in groups, slide into pose, and being sons of mothers and brothers to sisters maintained the fifties silence so eloquently practised by their war-zoned fathers on soldier settlements stretching to the horizon, not quite, pockets of square miles, identical houses, drainage channels reclaim swamps into hay fields and clover, paspalum, patterson's curse — there are stories to the names — out of Bathurst, of the burr of the same name, there are hills and fields of salvation jane and a prison razed in the riot in '79 and there is the place north-west of Lithgow where Frank Nugan was found dead in his car. The trigger pulled. The gun goes off. Pop. Heads resound. Panic. Notes are found. A list of names surfaces briefly, quickly drowns. A most important scandal this and the telling of it seems to go backwards, gets foggy, muddled as time passes and secrets get buried meticulously in commissions and reports, bits and pieces of a marvellous story told by obfuscation, denial and absurdity.

Mary Stevens will tell you how hard it is to know what's going on when the crucial company records are either absent or written in code. (Why doesn't she use the word corruption?)

Merchant banks are grand illusions, soap opera set-pieces with marble lobbies and plate glass. We are not meant to believe in merchant banks or CIA agents or bright young men in slick suits with only a bar for a filing cabinet and their fingers in every pie. It's all for sale. Numbers ideas brains contacts covers telexes receipts dates the time of day. They stand smiling at the crossroads of the political and the economic. Lawyers guns and money. Do ya wanna buy? Sell? Set up? Hide? Here's my card. Give us a call. Just say the word. We'll do business. I respect (your) principles.

In this scene the spirits are bottled and the self-reflections are mirrored. Irving Stone is an addict of both, or so this role decreed

— Hilton Hotel Businessman this year, Bahrain, Delhi, Tokyo, Hong Kong, Singapore. Or so the passport said.

'No one spends more than a week in Singapore and this stamp says six months. Must have been some girl.' Stone looked shocked, looked down, said 'She was,' catching the inquisitor's eye, not saying 'How do you shadow a bank, tail a trail of fifth-floor office suites or bug eight buildings in eight different countries and watch your own back?'

Stone was tired. Almost too tired to spar with Martins. The politician could have been playing any game. Stone had no reason to suspect him. Of what? Knowing things? Lilywhite front men called politicians, they are determinedly rotten detectives. What can they afford to know? Stone decided to ignore. Martins persisted.

'We have a very special relationship. Us. With the US. An intimacy that occurs rarely in our more human existence. Some call it strong and certainly there is power. Do you take my meaning Mr Stone? The free world as we call it is a complex place. We cannot have everything perfect all the time, in fact the tensions, the imperfections, the push, the pull, they make new synthetics, energy . . . (smoke screens) . . .'

Stone interrupted, 'Really Martins, isn't that rather histrionic? As you can see I'm a British citizen and as such outside the fold of the Australian–American romance. Was there another point to your eloquence?'

Martins. A Country Party member. A minor electoral performer but still *au fait* with the game. He puzzled like a bank teller, methodical and intransigent, 'Computers Mr Stone, a booming line of work you're in. You sell?'

'Design.'

'Ah. The princes of the future my advisers keep telling me. The key holders. Power brokers. (The might of push button, the right of colour television.) I am intrigued Mr Stone. What does a computer design engineer do in Alice Springs for four months?'

What indeed!

2

It is a mystery

Joan. Daughter of the Damascus Sheets and Towels Company, Tocumwal 1904–1952 (the company not Joan). Rural capitalism. Boarding school in Melbourne. A deb in '36. Married a year later to young Harold Blair (Bob) Stevens — student, from a good family, off to a Ph.D. at Cambridge, she kept up with the whisky and cigarettes and the curious constraint of an academic wife. The war. Fascism. Pacifism. The arguments were certainly lively and she engaged over tea with the women at work and studied the lessons of the revolution in Spain as she studied French and literature at a nearby women's college. When the war finally came Joan got a job carrying mail between bureaucracies (they had moved up to London). Not a bad job at all, lots of exercise walking or bicycling about the lanes and courtyards of the government section of town. She spent six months out at Fensham Woods when they moved the special communications and children away from the blitz. It was nice in the country in summer and autumn. When Joan returned to Bob and the flat near the London School of Economics, a rather beautiful dark-haired person with ruby lipstick and rare black stockings had moved in. 'Sally, this is Joan, my wife. Sally will be staying for a while.' Joan immediately applied for another country post. Shropshire for the duration, the business of cracking codes.

It occurred to Joan many times that she loved Bob and would do anything. He could do anything, she didn't mind, but he didn't want her anymore. It was brutal and she clamoured for him, believing in sexual healing. Bob and Joan made love once, twice, several times before the geographical end. She argued, begged, pleaded that it could work, that they could all live together. Bob tried to talk to her, to argue back, to be gentle and verbal but he invariably snapped; she would repeat a gesture and he would snap with anger and contempt. He told her forty times over he didn't love her and then they made love and he stayed all night and she looked contemptuously at him over the cowardly breakfast he had accepted because he was hungry, because she was his wife.

Bob and Sally and Joan postponed the disintegration of the ménage. They travelled together on the boat back, Bob and Sally getting off at Perth for a new start, Joan staying on as far as Melbourne, going home.

Mary Stevens was born in Melbourne in July, 1946.

By the way

After the war they organised water for the dry land and settled soldiers and refugees and migrants there. Griffith and Colleambally, an unlikely oasis, a European place in the inland of the oldest continent, made green and productive by water carried in open channels across the dry country, flourishing, the generosity of a land so responsive to the white attention, so devastated by their ignorance, wilfulness. Here they made their artificial place rather grand if you do not measure ambition in millennia, Ayres Rock and the scarp of Arnhem Land.

Burke and Wills (and a forgotten third person named King who survived by being cared for by the hostile Aborigines) went through this area a hundred years before and marvelled at the heaven's display, the wide sky, the shooting stars, the comets, the planets, Mars and Venus leaping into view. It all seemed so much closer then, and more mystical. They lay on their groundsheets and heard the camels snore, watched the brilliant sky fold colour on colour as the sun went down. They were happy then, adventurers failing to see the omens. They died a year or so later, becoming martyrs then to the landscape and to the landscape of their fantasies.

A man called Tony Naismith escaped from a Griffith childhood and the fifties, at the earliest opportunity, taking off for Sydney and a job in a bank, studying accounting at night — he never intended going back. (He's the structural flaw in this book.)

By 1976 Naismith was known as single-minded, determined, fanatical in a quiet sort of way. He declined alcohol and cigarettes until you remembered not to ask and took to having orange juice, mineral water and milk in the fridge. He had an excellent brain.

Highly ordered, like a filing cabinet, indexed and photographic with the added bonus of mathematics. He read computer manuals in bed but never trained, he was a natural of a unique sort.

He was young, energetic, clean, like an American, but unhampered by that arrogance. Chance. The right place at the right time. Historical accident. The official blind eye. Several things combined to produce Tony Naismith. An elegant apartment. Money moved as at a table game. By cleverness he amassed a sort of wealth both conspicuous and hidden, every inch the successful businessman, the paradigm who could manufacture self-righteousness in Canberra when aspersions were cast. Sources of cash flow? The amount of tax owing? His bluster worked well. Our modern day superman played squash with the senator and flew back to Sydney for a celebratory lunch with the staff. But this was a preliminary skirmish. The hounds stuck to the trail. Enemies are everywhere for those who owe so many favours and eventually he had to run.

He skipped the country one Sunday evening, never to be seen again, or not until Sarah and Edith floated down the Matterhorn and saw a chap fall in front. They helped him up and behind the layers and goggles there was a familiarity, a seventies memory, and they went each their own ways. That was in 1982.

As luck and fiction would have it Stone also saw Naismith, in '79. A surprise in the bar of the Canberra Rex. The sort of surprise that only comes to two men who recognise each other's disguise.

They could play a game here, a double game, for who could say, spontaneously, who had the most to lose, or whether in fact, this confusing coincidence was predetermined or cosmic or something else?

They had both come up in the world from those stuffy nights in the Glebe Motel with its waving palms dying even at the beginning of the drought and the red neon that was on all night and made you thankful you'd been given a back room that looked toward the sunset, a pollution red sky crossed by airplanes, soundless at this distance, like a postcard of a city that went west forever and made you want to just fly.

Naismith hid out here before he left the country? drowned? turned? had a face-lift? disappeared? went to live in South Africa? Take your pick, the official versions make even less sense.

And such a talented man might fill lost years with many things. Tony kept his hands in. Jamaica. Saudi Arabia. The Bedouins. Pragmatic living in the desert with tribes of stark belief and greater strength. A sort of peace.

Later, on an Israeli kibbutz, camouflaged as chook-plucker and water-carrier, Naismith got fit and healthy and aggressive again. A quick deal on the high seas and the Israeli generals and Colonel Qadaffi are both smiling. These days it's that sort of war.

The Glebe Motel was Amelia's idea of deep cover for her boy Stone. She had placed him there, down the end of the trendy-dero-student suburb, proximate to Naismith and all the rest, the container terminals and tug-boat milieu, a stone's throw from racetracks where money launderers stepped out of the night and drove their Mercedes along the canal as if the success of their task required clandestinity. Stone stayed for as long as he could bear it, a month, six weeks. He watched Naismith load the suitcases of files and cash into the back of a taxi, listened to the radio announce another Royal Commission, lay on Bondi Beach to get the tan he was vain enough to want to take back to the northern hemisphere and winter and the waiting patiently for the end of these preparations (and the beginning of the job).

Some things known about Tony Naismith
He was in Edith's memory too. Briefly, in the seventies sometime, Edith and Cecil had been entrée to the conspicuous consumption set who liked to patronise the arts, or at least invite them to cocktail parties and laugh over wine, buy a painting or two, small sketches mostly. Nothing flashy about Naismith though he always enjoyed openings immensely. A sense of occasion descended over him and he would look about, eager, personable and candid. Edith remembered him as a sober young businessman who talked to you rather than with you, who knew the limits of his wit and liked as much to listen, nodding at other's conversational gymnastics.

Cecil had even been invited to several events and once he and Edith caught the public bus to Palm Beach where everyone thought them very quaint to have thought of it, 'What an adventurous life you poets must lead, we might just try it sometime,' standing aloft the cliff face in brilliant houses perched like breathlessness on the ocean view. A cocoon. This was Tony Naismith's place. Or seemed to be. He was almost a host. There were drinks with waiters on the terrace and then Mrs Naismith, never before sighted, graced a complete formal dinner table in high summer. The guests drank champagne cocktails which, Cecil muttered, was a waste of good champagne, and ate strawberries before sitting down to a traditional Christmas fare complete with Grace (the prayer not the person).

Also out of Griffith

A hundred miles or so south, closer to the Murray than to any other landmark, a large property, dry land. Grace had lived there all her life.

She had learned from the land to drive a hard bargain. Patience. To pay attention. To work. To be capable, behind doors closed against the conventions, to determine her own life. Her heart could harden and the men on the property conceded. It was easier, they'd say, deciding her strength was the exception that proved their rule.

Grace lived at a fast pace, thoroughly. It was known she was intellectual, also obsessive, a good worker, as good as any man, also extremely silly after two Pimms and liable to sing off-key.

Grace's children succeeded. The land she worked with her husband Stanley made the brightest green, the tallest oat. Mares foaled at sensible hours, the chooks laid all year round, they kept bees in the orchard and they bottled fruit in the late evenings of autumn. So why did it cross her mind, the question, what place the anger in this neat world?

Stanley never thought about or minded his wife. She just was, and he was more entertained than puzzled when she would ask questions, out of the blue, could he remember what had become of Cyril Naismith's boy, you know, the one that went off to Sydney, comes home every five years or so in a fancy car? And sure enough, the next time he saw Cyril at the Lodge young Tony's name came up and Grace could put that part of the puzzle down.

3

Patience is a handy skill for a spy

The hen's party, as the men called it. Some of the best brains in the country. The cream of the forties. Striding on from the war. Joan back from England with a child. Amelia arriving. Sarah set up nicely thank you, a pretty family of two girls, lucky her. And Grace had produced a doctor and then a nurse, she allowed herself to glow with upward mobility although she didn't often talk about Johnny who was a farm-hand and did the hay and then the cannery and went to Queensland for the winter and anonymous adventures. He was good with horses. She wondered when he would settle down.

The hen's party. Four minds focused on the matter. Those minds. That youth. That beauty captured by box Brownie snaps. The uncoventionality. The success. Here, in 1956, a coven shipwrecked by a tidal wave of complacency, their own or that of their times, wool was a pound for a pound and would never be that again. (To be in your thirties and watching the world change before your eyes. They could reach back and touch the generations before. Memory contained that which culture, the institutions, the necessities of ideology, would manage in a decade to erode. And unless something happened, they would collaborate.)

They had never stopped meeting writing phoning visiting talking exploring exploding the detail and the diabolic; by '56 it looked like history or something, TV, the Olympic Games, the Great Flood on the Murray, had stranded their sorcery, the power of group. They had become tense, tight, floundering about on the new vinyl chairs, spilling milk in drops on occasional tables made these days in odd shapes, neither square nor round nor anything resembling utility (decoration had overwhelmed), they jerked and tilted over the tea cups. (The scones were tasteless. Sarah had left out the salt.)

It was Joan (being a school-teacher) who set the ball rolling, got the train back on the tracks, set them off on new paths through the bush. She set them a problem, a puzzle, a matter at the same time theoretical and make-believe. For solution they would collect: information and thoughts; intuitions and knowledge (and prejudices) then meet again in a month. Afternoon teas became something rather different. This would last for thirty years.

At first it was provincial and rather gossipy — land ownership, balance of trade, Government House garden parties and the influence of old school tie, the sort of hard stuff (facts) that can be got from uncles in the right places and a quick look at the social pages. It was an (endless) game.

The years marched on. So did their sophistication. Year books, budgets, annual reports, bookmakers' records, obscure publications, press clippings, the cabin trunk bulged. They had a very good day at the races in 1964 and bought a little company. They learned how to put it together and by 1969 they had spun a web world-wide: holidays in Jerusalem and Dominica, Geneva and New York. . .they contrived eccentricity, created their existence in a wider world, poised and patient, they waited to spring the trap.

Hard to believe?
Consider if I had written it this way.
Given you this information.
Which is also true.

Sarah was married eighteen years to Arthur, high salary, management, brand new house with enormous rooms. She mothered, kept house, organised the cleaning and shopping, entertained the businessmen, putting them up in the spare rooms overnight with matching sheets and towels fresh from the linen press. A woman came once a week just to do the ironing. The businessmen came regularly over the eighteen years (later she analysed their distribution/incidence and it was not random). She got to know the names of hometowns and wives and children and accents and she fed them good baked dinners, fillet steak, turkey (once one October) and her grandfather's recipe for apple pie. And then her husband left her. Overnight. Suddenly. She knew she was vague but this was really a surprise. It seemed he took nothing but left a note, a clear intention, no questions. Then the house was burgled. Twice. Arthur's files and books and papers. The whole desk was taken the January long weekend she always spent at Guerella.

Sarah had the house burglar-proofed and bought a dog (a chow) and wondered, nagging at herself, what she had done to deserve this. She floated off, eventually, into the Australian weather, the skies and summers and journeys. One day she heard a man speak at a conference, a radical chap whose role it was to rant a bit and raise the consciousness of the assembled 'middle class professionals'. He spoke a list of names and dates, coincidences, he made a case more fanciful than true but some of the names rang familiar, stirring Sarah's memory and making her make the sense, security agents, industrial espionage, simple statements of patronage, research scholarships, directors of the board, mineral surveys and handy light planes. The names rang. All those cheerful Americans eating off *her* best dinner plates, Arthur's business partners turned masked men and Arthur a husband who, amongst other things, lied forever. This made her feel sick all over again until she remembered, focused. Now she had the names, aliases and allies, some use could be made of this.

And this information

Amelia had been married once. It was after the war. In France. And only briefly, not even a reception, Francesco had had to leave suddenly, the police. He'd reappear fifteen years later but by then Amelia would have done fifteen years of other things: a nightclub dancer on the Côte d'Azur (of course); a migrant (America first then Canada then Australia). She had at least two passports and Francesco had gone to gaol for five hundred thousand francs worth of heroin, so she had that much worth of invisibility, and she worked: cleaner (domestic and industrial); typist (the French Embassy and then the United Nations); receptionist (at a local factory); book-keeper (at another factory); researcher (for various government departments); childminder; hairdresser (of average ability and somewhat terrifying ambition); teacher (of French and thus she met Joan); altogether a mixed bag of skills and handy infiltrations.

Amelia was a sort of widow and an escape-artist of means. Certainly she witnessed the Americans organise the mafia to beat up the communists in Marseilles in 1946. And the rest. She owned a terrible ambition for more than haircuts.

4

In this particular company

It was Amelia's idea to professionalise their pastime. Their research had left them few books to read, few stones unturned, they sat on the brink of obviousness. Redundancy threatened. Amelia arrived back from overseas aglow with plots and possibilities, reality, fantasy, a set of secret companions found, a rather nice maybe-German woman who believed their expertise might be of great use, if they were serious...

'Well are we?'
'Yes.'

There was much to talk about. Credentials. Ideology. Whose side and what if and is there any danger? To replace the game. To act. To make the cosseted brains work. This was something best left to fantasy or to novelists. Sarah nodded. Smiled. 'Why not? At worst we can be wrong and so won't affect. At best we are correct. Might make a difference. Besides. I'm getting on for sixty. There is no point in living carefully.'

'How shall we?'

They met in cities.
Centrality. Anonymity. The constancy of sound. The illusion of public privacy. Like many others they used impersonality, the alienation, conventionality, for clandestinity.

Joan's cabin trunk of chaos and filing cards was moved into the extra room built on the back verandah of her Footscray house. One weekend Amelia and Sarah did the finishing and painting. Grace had done the special wiring and they needed to plaster over the tell-tale signs of thick cable, extra earth. Then the Telecom men could install the extension telex from the company. This was quite legal and gave Joan a pleasant sensation of legitimacy. She telexed the office. The switch-girl answered with her everyday humour. The lines were open.

The computer came next and that was unsettling. Joan had grown fond of the cabin trunk painted pale blue and standing upright in a corner. It held in little draws on neat filing cards hand-written in spider's scrawl the body of their knowledge and the intricate interrelations that they had made between the 'random' and the 'innocent'. The cross-reference system was indecipherable to Amelia (who never stayed around long enough to become familiar). Joan and Sarah held the keys in their heads and that seemed good enough and safer than some electronic brain that had no discrimination and was vulnerable to any deft hand at a keyboard.

To be serious was to take bigger risks. The computer was small, compact, it belied the risks it invited. Joan was reluctant. Grace insistent. Together they melded technology and chaos into a confusing if not foolproof arrangement of locks and keys and fall-backs and warnings (and raids on the Government and defence department and anything else they could get the entry codes to, but they didn't like to talk about that). Joan was placated. A computer programmed with idiosyncrasy suited her better. She set about giving over her precious file cards and kept the blue trunk intact in her bedroom, under the bed. She had to work late into the night to keep the double system up to date.

The takeover came next. Their little company with its staff of fifty and its warehouse of spare parts, electronic gadgetry and kitchen applicances was swept with anticipation. Flarenhof Mechanical, a Swiss concern, had made the offer on paper. Typists and accountants became concerned. Would they lose their jobs? What about the valuable local contacts, the reputation for efficiency and personal service? The tension grew.

Stone (renamed Roche for this occasion) swept in one balmy Melbourne morning with an entourage of blue suits and brief-cases and eyes that watched and mouths that didn't speak above a whisper in his ear. The new owners. Real coffee was made in the silver service. Susan on the switch sent out for lunch and a fine bottle of Scotch. The boardroom air became heavy with smoke and sweat and the feeling of being on the line.

One by one the managers and assistants, the foremen and storemen, came for their appointments, answered the questions, explained the reports they had hurriedly assembled for these foreign gentlemen (and one woman). At the end of the day no one had lost a job, several people had been promoted and it became clear that the sleepy suburban company of Brevitt and Soames was about to become an arm of some amorphous global concern.

Two of the blue-suited gentlemen stayed, installed in a hastily refurbished storeroom. They hired extra girls for the paper-work and truckloads of hardware arrived, the property next door was acquired and life at the office took on, for Susan at least, the air of capitalist adventure. Her telexes now went out to Europe and Hong Kong, she had to work back to send them in the appropriate time zones, new files were created and grew, the safe was installed, the coffee consumed, and the growing parade of unfamiliar faces made her facilitating role even more so.

By the end of six months the handsome Mr Roche departed, leaving, as he said to Susan on his last day over lunch at Florentino's, the business in her capable hands. She was to become manager of the Australian operation, someone with complete discretion, at double the salary of course. Susan's common sense muffled the suspicion in her stomach, she accepted, responsible directly to Joan Stevens, the mousy woman who seemed rather to potter than to actually know anything. Susan saw the sense of her own efficiency being bought, she asked for and got full superannuation, six weeks' holiday a year and exclusive use of the company car. She was no fool. She had watched the parochial go international and while she might not comprehend she knew at many other levels that large things were occurring. If she was valuable they could pay for it. One needs proper bribes to keep one's eyes and mouth closed.

Simultaneously the city cradled the conspirators. The constant background noise disguised their talk. And in the silence (those moments when only the wind is heard), that silence harboured.

Women's talk. Women's work. Any city cradles conspirators.

Each worked alone travelling the conventional routes, they'd rendezvous and depart, exchange passwords, wear complex badges of identity: Susan's pink socks said all clear, Sarah's beige suit said urgent, the brown was for no contact, Joan set pot-plants on the verandah and forgot to take the rubbish in, Amelia sat in the window at Pellegrini's smoking Gitanes, Grace met her promptly at six in the State Library newspaper room. The domed ceiling could amplify their words, they worked at opposite sides of the table, openly, each adept at gazing seriously into space and reading upside down.

The professionals moved confidently, paid attention to detail: the transportation of apparatus (packing for the three weeks at Guerella every summer), the sheltering and feeding of travellers (it was about time Amelia transcended jet lag or stayed in one place a bit longer), the time for sleeping and talking, the peculiar process that is not premised in briefcase and hotel lobby. So much public ground inaccessible (or clichéd to this game, and dangerous), they skirted the pillared hallways, sat in coffee shops in art galleries, made conversation in ordinary places, travelling regularly on the same bus to work (or so it seemed for a week or two). They went to the movies in twos on wet Sunday afternoons and for a while, a few months, Joan and Sarah took season tickets to the Proms, getting the work done at interval, program notes, heads bent over photographs of holidays and grandchildren; an article in the latest Fabric Studies Journal; they might enrol in a course. They had been at it so long. It was second nature. And they knew. It wouldn't be their skill that failed. Or their assumptions?

5

In which we meet Mary Stevens

When Mary Stevens left Australia in 1976 she abandoned a myriad of detail and incident that might have informed her, had she paid attention to it, of her fate. As it was, she returned in 1983 (the seven year gap in which politicians and other crooks let the inquests and investigations and appeals and commissions do their languid stuff, had occurred and it was all over the press, on everyone's lips — conspiracy, corruption, courts. By then the lawyers-guns-and-money line had a decidedly seventies ring about it).

Susan Miller was seventeen (on page 2) in 1957. Her career would be decided and pursued with natural efficiency and in the context of affluence. Remember full employment? Blonde hair and red nail polish fitted her perfectly for many positions. A spell as receptionist in Collins Street served her well in her more off-Broadway performances. She worked summers at the beach resorts in Victoria and came back to town in March, a new year, a new job. A way of varying the otherwise predictable world she was bound for.

Susan first came across Mary Stevens in a boarding house in one of those suburbs noted only for such establishments, corner shops, cafés plain and open early, peak-hour trains. Actually they never met, weren't introduced, comfortable in anonymity they remained familiar faces, numbers on a letter box, a sneaked look at the name on a postcard.

They met properly four years later. Stevens worked downtown at Simms and Hillman, reputable dealer in credit ratings, divorce details, company directorships and other prized currencies.

Susan was 27 in 1967. Her career was decided and pursued with a natural efficiency in the context of 1960s affluence. Remember full employment? In ten years her clothes had changed, there was a decent salary, less time for shopping, passion spent elsewhere.

As an assistant to Henri Mathews (of Mathews, Maher and Milsom, Law/Accounts) Susan entered and left various buildings in the course of a working week. She had a way with lifts and their attendants, was on first-name terms with receptionists and was call-number familiar with telex operators, knew her way telephonically and by extension into several of the bureaucracies (Treasury, Supply, Finance, Taxation), the stock exchange, two of the three major banks, the airport, the Customs Department; and socially, the major daily newspaper, the prison, the markets. She kept her address book in code, lived mostly alone or in boarding houses and got along quite nicely.

For many years this period of Mary Stevens' life remained a blank. Few noticed her then, and those who did found reasons of their own not to mention it. Mary herself only spoke of these years when she was drinking and out of her class. Then she would tell amusing stories, humour working off the incongruity of this now-fast smart spy once putting brandy in her afternoon instant coffee and spiriting photocopies out the door in knitting patterns, the Whole Earth Catalogue and prints of the Australian Impressionists purchased in a lunchtime dash down St Kilda Road to the Art Gallery.

St Kilda Road. That gracious thoroughfare from the central business district to the seedy seaside suburbs, the freeways and beyond, the ruling class holiday cottages (as they liked to label them) at Portsea, a weekender with marble floors and panelled wood walls, and solid bluestone, so good for the harsh summers. Susan Miller drives down to this house with the dictaphone and some papers for Henri, to return the next day with a week's work for the typing pool and the assistant secs, and a flexi-day to add on to her own vacation due at the end of February, when the season changes.

Mary Stevens is here, moonlighting during the four week annual, chief cook and bottle-washer to the Mathews family (oh, and of course, driving the children). Mary made a cup of tea for the girl from the office in the same way that she had found herself making coffee and fruit juice and even drinks before dinner, playing at maid, keeping the toilet clean, the washing machine regular, the

ironing in a fresh pile by the laundry door. She made Susan and Henri a pot of Russian Caravan and as she unloaded the tray she placed the face, and put it to the familiar voice. Where. The face. Sydney. A few years back. Voice. Melbourne. Just last week. (A coincidence.)
Mary Stevens went out to the kitchen and poured herself a cup of Lanchoo (she was going through a very class-conscious phase with all this playing at maid). She filled the sink with the steaming water and added lemon liquid soap. Susan Miller brought the empty cups out and stood leaning against the back door in the afternoon sun.
'You used to live at Miss Tree's boarding house in Redfern a few years back, we used to pass on the stairs.'
Stevens smiled, introduced herself. She held back the I'm-only-doing-this-to-save-money-for-overseas speech and heard Susan Miller's name instead, and more:
'You're the woman on extension 413 aren't you? I've always wondered who Henri's mysterious source on matters less than legal was. Do you take any risks?'
'It's just part of the job. Perfectly legal. I take certain calls. As long as a set of one of the five code words are used, I'll tell the caller anything. I imagine they pay a lot for the privilege. At most I'd get ten of those calls a day, you know, on special occasions, like the stock market boom or an escalation in Lebanon. I believe it's a somewhat randomised security system, all anonymous. There are five girls taking calls, the numbers are given out up top. I don't even know the full number, that's why we say "Special Information speaking". What *is* the number by the way?'
'2828413'
'Simple. I might use it myself one day though I guess they change the number when a girl leaves. Do they?'
'Yes. But give me a ring at Henri's office. Susan Miller. We might be of use to one another. I'd better get back to the desk. He's a bloody boss. I'm real glad he's down here. Don't envy you the 24-hour-a-day stuff. How's it going?'
'It's only for a month. The money is OK and I do get to go to the beach. Saving to go O.S. you see.'
'Yeah. Good luck. Maybe I'll see you again.'
'Bye.'

By the time Mary Stevens had left the department of special information, by the time she had amassed the three thousand a girl needed to have in those days before departing the shores of our distant continent, Susan Miller had been gone from Henri Mathews' office for months. During this time she had interviewed many prospective employers, settling finally for a small firm that seemed to offer a great deal of work and responsibility. She was looking for something different, easier than the perfect grooming and manners brigade she had found it necessary to join in order to learn the ins and outs of business management. Joan Stevens caught her interest immediately by asking 'Why on earth does someone like you apply for a job in a commercial backwater like this (meaning Footscray)? You could work in Canberra or North Sydney.' 'You said in the ad that you wanted someone who could run an office, staff, machines, schedules, orders, I may only be a secretary but I can certainly do that, and better than any middle-management man.'

They talked on. Yes, Joan was one of the directors but she didn't work there. The place ran itself from the warehouse floor. Always. The last girl had had to leave suddenly (married unfortunately). She would see what turned up in the mail but for now Susan Miller could start on Monday. To be reviewed in a month.

Susan Miller started work as receptionist/secretary of the 'company' on the Monday Mary Stevens made the final payment on the return ticket to London via Athens. They were not to meet again until 1983 but Susan Miller let her summer curiosity and the strange coincidences and the expediency of boarding houses for working girls in ambitious jobs, take her back to irregular residence at Miss Tree's over the next seven years, on and off, where she heard around the never-changing kitchen table the conversations that pass on information about long-gone people despite their steadfast refusal to send postcards or even remember. Mary Stevens was so talked about. She never sent postcards there but she did remember. She turned up to stay for few weeks in March 1983. Her return was taken as a matter of course and hardly commented upon, until she was gone again without collecting the years of mail accumulated in the dark boxes that hung in the hallway.

The night the helicopters circled and circled the city. Just past full moon. No pretence of covert. That is how we know. Multiplier effect, political economy, at any point in time that which is, is twenty times more than what we know.

What is dramatic here, now? The office workers? The girls in boarding houses? Ghosts? Ghosts in Paraguay, yes. But not Redfern. Not Moonee Ponds. These days of Fraser government, a squeezing of the breath, perhaps that digging in, settling for ground maintained, cut your losses, continuance. Continue until it is over, this deepening economic crisis, this time when all that was exciting is ground down by repetition and responsibility; plans are made to flee. The flight is subtle and threatens to become ephemeral. Struggle does not rest on mere belief. Continuance requires many acts of danger and boredom, the ordinary. The known can be enough. It all depends. On random factors. On process. On people's lives. On the fascination with culture, which is where both crime and politics should accurately reside. There. The night the helicopters circled and circled the city. Just past full moon. That is how we know.

6

The Glebe poets

All over Glebe (or any other inner-city self-conscious suburb proximate to university and the working class) lone poets in their single rooms, pouring coffee listening 'metaphorically' to the sirens screaming, beginning at once (and in unison) to transform
> When they come for us puffed up, sweating
> look to science fiction
> the literary imperative of prison...

They are lonely but would not at all enjoy each other's company where alcohol and speeches would deflate the word pictures. In the sounds of the trees, the wind, they each hear the present rushing by without them. They phone an old friend and go to the Cross for (more) coffee and crowd-watching, eavesdropping their way into the real world.

Tonight the Glebe poets are all out drinking red wine and making jokes. The rooms of the Glebe poets are empty. Dark boxes of postponed urgency. Cockroaches left to play amongst the coffee dregs and manuscripts, the bins of crumpled paper...

This is Alan's room. He sometimes worries about the number of trees he 'consumes'. Tonight he is not worrying about trees. He is on his way to a party after cleaning his teeth vigorously while the cool breeze through the louvres propped up his senses. There will be girls to be offered lifts home, a nice night for sharing a bed and in the morning she could listen as he reads his latest efforts, takes vitamin B with herbal tea, some classical music, achievements in anticipation, another successful sexual and poetic interlude.

Alan anticipates. He does not recall last Sunday. It rained all day to the point where everyone but the academics (who have well-behaved children and only one of each sex) and poets (who have no children at all) had been out getting wet and enjoying it.

Alan listened to the football results and contemplated a journey to a hot-dog. He is able to see the folly of this. The poem he writes tonight will be ironic but soft. He lets his mind run on through the wet afternoon, it came to a familiar fantasy, his imagined scores of illegitimate offspring. (Were the sum of lovers less than that? Perhaps some had twins.)

Alan was a determined person (some called him stolid but clearly they lacked imagination), with desires more rampant than his actions. Alan invented unknown sons and daughters in order to imagine seminal meetings. Of course, incest, the saving fantasy of middle-aged men, or the attraction of young women, is not so fine as mid-life crisis or so noble as the reasonable fear of growing old and doddering around, forgotten in a nursing home. Worse than dying. After he turned thirty-five Alan imagined any young woman as his long-lost daughter. He was more selective about his sons. So he took to the kids down the Cross (watching them from coffee shops), he would find mannerisms and nose shapes to validate his parenthood and in the early morning, in the still-dark world and the yellow-lit room, the coffee brewing, the surreal percolating, the ambition flowing like ink from his treasured leaky fountain pen, Alan would flower, satiated with harmlessness, newspapers and the memory of last night which had been poets and red wine and feminist students still dancing to loud music at three in the morning.

A Particular Last Night

Alan had slept till midnight in order to front at Mitch's do, sparkling in a black satin cloak lined with mauve, rain dripping from his curls. He made an entrance. Mitch laughed, disdainful and pitched him a line from one of Alan's own poems:

and so the warriors were wrought
in pastel pink
pale blood sports

Alan hadn't cringed or blushed. He counted on no one recognising the rhyme. He replied, 'It is absurd to pretend that writing, the art of scratching, is important, or anything but elitist, perhaps so small as to be, merely, the definition of clique and cliché.' He completed the poem

and cranes
like dinosaur skeletons revived

grinding and whirring
a chap proportioned to tiny brain
swings levers like a ghost train
going nowhere
the scrapers are tombstones from the future
erected now to make sure.

Girls nodded. Poured wine, Lit cigarettes. Talked in low voices, laughing. Attractive pictures. Alan ceased reciting, the men might have heard it before. He could no longer remember the details, the script of the pose. The rooms filled with smoke and music. Conversations and bodies swirled familiar and it was as if he knew everybody and they had always been arranged thus, ah, the early morning calm of being held safely in the arms of party games.

Alan smirked and cracked one-liners, after three polystyrene cups of red the lines came fast enough and needed less cleverness to raise a laugh. 'Gees, Baxter's a bit over the top, off the air, out of it over there shouting and falling about on the couch.' The girls swayed back and turned a degree or two away. This was Alan's cue, alcohol brave, to slide in and compete, make clear his relative superiority as a man; good ones, he knew, were hard to find.

Arlene arrived. She arrived at the party after Alan, after Baxter had flaked snoring in a corner, after all the peanuts had gone. She chatted low with a couple of people she knew, rolled a large joint around the kitchen table with Mitch's dope and asked Alan to drive her home. In the car she said,
'Do you live alone? I hate all this false flirting and seduction. Are you interested in spending the night. Let's go to your place, as they say on the radio.'

Alan, overcome by the ease of it all, readily agreed, Arlene was equally pleased. The guy was easy, no bother, she could turn him on, give his ego a shot, it was a bed, maybe, for a couple of nights and Arlene was desperately in need of a place to sleep.

She had been working nights and was wrung out by no money, landlords, junkies, and the rest. The big life had mashed her, pummelled the talent and ambition into grit and cast-iron. Alan was a mild-mannered creep which was better than a macho or a really creepy creep. Temporarily (again) without house or home, fleeing from another abortion, another broken heart, the confusion of being wrong, again, of looking round months, years on, and seeing nothing gained. An offer to sing in a club for beer and tips and 'something more if it goes OK' was as low as you could go but she had gone there. The pale skin of night work turned white under fluorescence and the stares of men dribbling beer down chins; you can see why Arlene loved Alan easily, he was relative, an artistic fuck, candlelight and Mozart, the grand movements propping up both their performances. He groaned and groaned. She heaved and sighed and opened her eyes. She gazed through the room and its rubble. God, she hated classical music. Constant reminder of her ignorance. Her presence. And her absence.

The wind came up pretending that the rain might clear tomorrow. Arlene was cheered by the wind, felt hunger, looked in the fridge, the cupboards, grilled cheese on toast. She would give anything for a plate of pasta, a roast chicken, a real ham sandwich even. At home, in her own home, she might have cooked a pie, an aubergine soufflé. The phone would have rung. Betty from across the street would have popped in for a cup of tea and a break from the kids and the football.

Arlene stayed at Alan's place for three days. She left with three first editions, signed by the authors. They'd make a few dollars. She arrived at the club early. Clean, showered, changed, rested. The green walls and yellow carpet skated away from her. The spotlight shadowed cheek and shoulder bone. Tonight she would sing the blues as never before, but the piano player didn't turn up and the disc-jockey did. Arlene sat at the bar smoking the barmaid's cigarettes one after another. Maybe not this time. Optimism. (How do *you* feel when you're so drunk, so out of it?) Yes, there definitely was a wind. Tomorrow or the next day she could lie topless on a blue-ribbon beach. Neilson Park. That was something to look forward to.

Arlene almost didn't get to the beach. Dysmenorrhea, depression, cigarettes, greasy sheets, but the room she slept in heated up unbearably by eleven, so she escaped on a hot bus and lay drowsing on the sand, baking away the awfulness.

Two perfect women spoke, complaining to each other (and the sand) about the difficulty of getting decent help these days. They sang loud intimacies, practised at ignoring the likes of Arlene who lay flattened and pulpy on her skinny towel. Fay and Deborah reclined on banana lounges, shining and neat, untouched by flies,

sand, children taken off by the girl from New Zealand. Arlene swam up and down in the blue sea. Revived. Listened to the soap-opera patter, suddenly found herself saying 'Excuse me,' (remembering her manners for the ruling class) 'I couldn't help overhearing. I'm an experienced private secretary, excellent references...', names dropped like diamonds on to cream buns, the sun sprinkled icing sugar over them, Fay and Deborah laughed quietly and let the girl talk, '...just got back from a position in Melbourne...old friend...starting her business...do you have a card? Perhaps I could phone you tomorrow. Couldn't begin until Thursday in any case, Mrs...?'
'Evans. Mrs Cecil Evans. Yes. Perhaps if you phoned, say at eight in the morning, We could...'

Arlene hurried to the bus-stop not daring to think. Had she brought it off?

She found Sal in the parlour at Surry Hills and hung around till she was through and they walked home together, patching up quarrels. Arlene was nervous about tomorrow but Sal was sick and Arlene made her garlic and lemon with hot water and whisky. Soon she could phone and know. The beginning or the end of comfort, complacency. To live with Sal again in that grim little house, hustling the boys for work of one kind or another, keeping your looks despite the night work and the anger and the dreary food and too much hard liquor. Sal drank all day these days and god knows what she got at the parlour. Arlene didn't ask. After the first couple of days she didn't ask, fearful really that the repulsion would fall away and she would find it easier than the Alans and Cecils of the world. Cecil Evans, Mrs Cecil Evans. Better get Mary to check them out at Simms and Hillman. Don't want to get taken for a ride by bankrupts or pretenders.

Arlene slept. Dreamed. Climbing climbing. Dreams of struggling upwards, clawing at clay and rock, running up hill, struggling from a pile of dead bodies dragging herself mouths and crotches and hand holds and toe holds the pile writhing and gangling grunting puffing bodies tumbling from above over and over blond curly hair a doll splayed on the footpath. The bodies turn to earth and waving grass smooth still warm from the sun though it is dark no moon Arlene is crouched panting on a grassy slope danger looms about her beyond the peak she is caught trapped unable to move the grass ripples in the wind moves waves and she is swimming striking out desperately though she has no idea what direction to take the waves come from all sides crashing on her. She is desperate but floating struggling to remain still calm. Eventually the sun will rise. I will at least be able to see the sky. It begins to rain. The stars disappear. Arlene is sinking. Dreaming within dreaming. She lets the rain trickle down her throat her arms her legs she is struggling crawling over sand collapsing. It is a sort of happy ending.

She wakes, dripping sweat of beer, of having survived. It is seven o'clock. The sun is up. The phone is waiting. She showers. Has breakfast. And the voice that answers is Fay, could she possibly begin today. A two week trial. Simply 'Yes,' there is no relief in the voice, 'I'll just bring one suitcase. We'll see how it goes.' Put the phone down. Grin. A sort of happy ending.

Arlene changed her name to Edith for her new job/new life. Just a year later she arranged to marry Cecil, despite Fay and the difference in their ages. She was not contacted when Sal was arrested at Asunción Airport, caught mid-way on a journey through that incredible maze: Hong Kong to Okinawa to Buenos Aires to Paraguay to Panama City to Los Angeles — traipsing along the commercial airways, smuggling drugs into the US of A.

Arlene/Edith heard nothing of this and Sal's subsequent death in a Paraguayan prison. And when she did hear it was hard for her to imagine she could have done anything. Sal had never been as strong or as bright. What did she expect? Going for the easy money. It was no good pretending. Now Edith firmly believed that we all have our choices to make (now she could afford to), that we cannot be responsible for the abuses of freedom our dead friends make. The bourgeoisie is not required to feel guilty. Besides, Cecil had to be in London for a reading in three weeks and she, of course, must organise.

7

Robbing the dead

There are banks.
Just that.
The bank.
'I'll have to see the bank and get back to you.'
'I'll talk to the bank about it, I'm sure we can do business.'
'I have to go to the bank, I'll meet you for coffee later.'
'I got held up at the bank, you know what it's like on pension day.'
'I had to go and talk to my bank manager, sorry I'm late.' The easiest of sentences. The liquid excuse.

The bank. From Hong Kong's merchant adventurers with their family empires in property, industry and shipping, and the growing financial ties with Peking, to Sal and the break that never came her way despite efficiency and courage, her gamble with the plate-glass world, the sort of crim networks the government departments know are too big to investigate.

There is dissonance in our language. The news reports tell us of another armed robbery. A desperate career and continuous with the myths stripped, by occurring on the six o'clock news, of romance. There is no romance in high finance. The legal crimes. The fortunes made and multiplied in the cleanest of ways. No jail to punish. No court to pry. Shuffle paper, burn and shred, run a million through the Barbados office and around the Pacific the trail will go cold.

8

The plot (I)

Based entirely on the notion that the world is a big place and truth stranger than fiction.

Mary Stevens has just returned from an accidentally extended tour of Paraguay. Two years before, misguided by the drunken exaggerations of an American journalist in a bar in L.A. (and the romanticism deposited in collective memory), Mary Stevens had booked an airline ticket to Mexico City, Acapulco, Brasilia and Asunción for two weeks thence. Mary Stevens had got drunk with the journalist and staggered through an uninspiring but pleasantly orchestrated fuck. He had a good record collection.

From Los Angeles she wrote a postcard.

Mary Stevens packed her one-of-each collection of essentials, panicked and bought three months' supply of vitamin pills, a fancy but inoffensive pocket knife and a ball of string from the nearest supermarket. She took herself to the airport and saw herself off to Mexico City.

Los Angeles. July, 1977.

Dear Mother,

leaving America in two days. There is something cloying about the yanks (esp. west-coast - by exhalting conformity, they guarantee weirdness. No - one can perform the dream. Guilty agoro becomes the norm. Hear Paraguay is something else. Will write long letter from there. It's OK travelling by myself, anything better than that dreary office. Trust school is as usual. Perhaps we'll go somewhere where they speak the french you so diligently taught me.

No more space. Keep well.

Luv Vlaicy

MRS JOAN STEVENS
41 MOORE ST
FOOTSCRAY HEIGHTS
VIC. AUSTRALIA.

AIR MAIL

Pearl Buck
USA 45c

Mary Stevens sank into Paraguay like a coin into a well, hopeful but lost to any ordinary purpose. Luckily Mary Stevens was an ordinary Australian girl. She had learned to swim. Rather well.

She free-styled her way into a whirlpool, the boudoir of an ageing Nazi who lavished fascist tastes on her and starred her in his esoteric and obsessive home movies (some few hundred feet still exist and are currently stored in the secret section of the National Library in Canberra). When discovered masturbating on her own time and for her own orgasm(s) Stevens was summarily demoted to floor-scrubber. For several months she learned knee-aching lessons in oppression and powerlessness and subsequently fell in love with Raoul the local lane-sweeper and head of the district revolutionary committee. Enjoined in struggle, Mary Stevens escaped the comfort of domestic labour and lived roughly in mud and timber huts and tin sheds with men and women who spoke no English and cared not at all that she was craving pop-up toasters and other equally incongruous trappings.

The lover affair with Raoul faded. It became clear that they would never drive victorious, standing side by side in the front seat of a liberated jeep, down the forest roads and into the main street of a free Asunción. Thus Mary, attired in woven shirt and trousers and a beanie made from a red and blue checked hillbilly shirt she had salvaged from a dead American, liberated the above-mentioned jeep and drove fast and hard to the nearest border crossing and into Argentina. Frying pans? Fire? No. Corrientes. A charming town. An outland. Mary walked with strong and confident stride (disguised desperation) into the nearest official building, the police station and liquor store.

Two bureaucratic days later Mary Stevens was finally taking a bath in an enjoyably plush hotel in Acapulco. That morning she had received a cheque from a New York trash newspaper and was busily rewriting her very ordinary history in order to do justice to the size of the advance payment offered almost offhanded for her stories from Paraguay. She soaked luxuriously, summarising whole decades into years and exaggerating brief encounters into profound political insights. She had no intention of disturbing the ethics of the press. She was not going to tell the truth.

The bath and self-analysis/deception were abruptly interrupted. A man and a woman. Both tall and sharply dressed. A superior-looking pair. She with late thirties confidence. He younger, an edge of handsome. They just unlocked the hotel room door and walked in. Casual. Detached. Unsurprised. The woman made a short phone call. The man seated himself in an armchair and lit a cigarette. The woman walked to the bathroom door.
'You should get dressed. I've bought you some clothes.'
Mary hoped the clothes were as smartly expensive as the woman's own. She fancied herself as generalised smart, unworried. The word appropriate flitted across her anxiety then vanished as she became aware of her ungainly naked dripping on the bathmat.
'Who are you?' she managed.
Introductions were made.
'Ian Stone'
'Dagmar Rock'
Ian Stone ordered scotch and gin on the telephone and addressed the room, the furniture, the two women and the waiter when he arrived a minute later. Mary listened to the catalogue of flight numbers, arrival and departure times, hotel bookings, lists of contacts and appointments, false names and rendezvous. Mary listened to this matter-of-factly-made invitation to work for the 'masters of world subversion' with a twinge of disappointment. The hotel had room service, four swimming pools, an all-night disco and a private beach. She managed to look bored. She felt bewildered. But she had learned something in the Paraguayan jungle. She gathered her passport and her two colleagues and made them take her shopping. Her plane left Acapulco for Shanghai at nine that night.

Acapulco. November. 1977.
Dear Mother,
      well it's been a long time I know and still I haven't room to explain. Two years. Will write in detail later. Just wanted to let you know Lin still alive. Paraguay. They say it's the worst country in the world. Landlocked. I was too. I knew only the history. It seemed romantic. The Jesuit experiments, pre-marxism (your influence), the Australian Utopian socialists going off to live the ideological life (Dad's contribution). The sharp contrast in geography. The landscape so um- Australian. It was stunning. No more space will continue

MRS JOHN STEVENS
41 MOORE ST
FOOTSCRAY HEIGHTS
VIC
AUSTRALIA.

/2.

Dear Mother (continued)

I imagined something could be concentrated there, been allowed to stay) or change (Romanticised it, didn't know anything about the haven for war criminals, the one hundred years of dictatorship, the corruption at customs, banks, the company, the blind eyes turned to collect percentages of laundered money and padded suit-cases, or the poverty. Perhaps all countries are like this but Paraguay exists for me as a symbol, a metaphor the nature of the state. My time there like the compulsory education of white western naivety. I learned a few things in Paraguay. The old men of Australians preserve the (old) culture of Lawson and God Abel so I conclude. The past is not always relevant.

Son Lewlfary

MRS JOAN STEVENS
41 MOORE ST
FOOTSCRAY HEIGHTS
VIC AUSTRALIA

Much later Mary Stevens was to say she remembered only one thing from China. Asleep one night in the guest room of a woman official at Ch'eng Tu she was startled awake by tiny feet running across her head, her face. Oh no, she groaned and leapt to the floor simultaneously flinging bedclothes in the air. She searched and searched and couldn't find the mouse anywhere, did deep breathing, fighting for calm over the irrational; she lay rigid on the bed and instead of giving up on sleep altogether climbed onto the cupboard there to sleep soundly safe until the woman official came in and, not finding guest or bedclothes, called out. Mary woke, said 'I'm up here', embarrassed now in the daylight. Her hostess was astonished. 'But my dear. There are no mice in China.'

If the world news services were remotely interested in telling us what is going on they would have told us about Mary Stevens' arrival in Hong Kong via (communist) China.

Mary, casual at a cat, walked across the border and climbed into a black limousine.

9

Points of view

Park Hotel Limited
Hong Kong
29.11.80

Dear Jan,

Today Robyn and I and Mary Stevens had afternoon tea at the Peninsular Hotel. Imagine if you can the last remnant of British colonial grandeur (in contrast to the totally thriving American glory which leaps out from every tiny shop front and street vendor), fighting a desperate rearguard action against the commercialism and crassness. Huge ornate Victorian tea rooms, immense ceiling all newly gilded, bell boys (in white of course), on each table a single long-stemmed rose and up in the little gallery a discreet chamber orchestra, all in dinner suits. Silver tea service. Very elegant. Delicious desserts, called ices, naturally.

We ran into Mary in the street. She approached us or I don't think I would have recognised her. She is no longer the plain little clerk at Simms and Hillman we all used to rubbish for working for the capitalists. Now she is vague and rather beautiful, seems to be surviving well enough. She had a car calling to take her to the Happy Valley Racetrack, so we cadged a lift (in a damned limousine if you don't mind, it made me quite queasy). The racetrack is on the floor of a steep valley but except for the successful punters (and the bookmakers) I suspect there isn't much that is terribly happy about the valley. Most of the people there live at a level of poverty the tourist pizazz fails to mention. There is no social security here. People sleep in the gutters and beg to sell you literally anything. The extremes of wealth and poverty are much more visible here than in Australia. The most rabid and hard-driving shopkeepers always have a small buddhist shrine on their valuable shelf space. We don't know the half about ambiguity and contradiction, not to mention the concept of the third world.

But I digress. Yes, we went to the races and we even won a little. Mary Stevens, of course, went to the members' enclosure and I got a glimpse of her now and again, seated in a private box with several important-looking and anonymously rich men and women popping in and out, languid or sinister smart, low key, suits so grey and understated that sunglasses are redundant.

Anyway. Enough of the torrid prose (just practising), I thought you'd like to hear about the Stevens encounter. You always liked her much better than I. We are having a wonderful and thought-provoking time. I hope you are well (and I wish you would finish the novel).

lotsa love
Carole.

Ah, so Mary Stevens is where the stakes are highest. The bets laid in diplomatic currency with brokers who use the word intelligence in a more than colloquial way and money changes hands with political rather than economic intent (if there is ever a distinction) and the outlaws, mobs and gangsters are not only above the law, they make it, are it, they keep it, their deadly privileged secret. Their dreams are melodramatic. Fitting. A murderous elite with power cool eyes.

Mary Stevens sipped her martini dry dry dry and listened to the cultured voices make small sentences. It is only in novels and paranoid fantasies that conspiracy theories hold any water. In life, in Hong Kong, in Happy Valley, in Peking, things are more relaxed, and more rational and, more than anything, to do with random factors.

Mary Stevens was rather sorry she had not asked the name of Carole's and Robyn's hotel. They were nice women and familiar. And they would have come in useful. Mary Stevens had some real work to do in Hong Kong.

10

The structure moves in response

The structure moves in response.
An agent of influence on/to the text.
The movement is planetary.
Various bodies orbiting a centre.
Tracked to fixed paths.
The relationships between the bodies change align and re-align eclipse and keep your distance.
There is occasional magic when the planets line up.
The sun moves.

Tony Naismith. Rapid fire action. A professional bender of rules for mercenary effect. Fighting fit. Doesn't drink or smoke.

Is married to a rose. A belle. A woman kept apart from the sordid, the economics. Rose Naismith signed here and here, traveller's cheques, gambling chits, traceable every step of the way for Rose Naismith never imagined, in fact knew to the contrary, she had anything to hide.

She also knew and was fond of saying '...to travel is to live'. To arrive, to depart, the expectation, to be packing for the journey, to be studying and making guesses at the weather, to be settling into a cottage for the summer or a villa for the winter or a pensione in the spring, an apartment by the ocean, whatever. Rose took houses apartments rooms long enough to settle in, to make arrangements for the next move, never long enough to acquire disappointment. Three months was the longest she had stayed in one place in years, though she returned to some places, her mother's, the villa in Spain, year after year, to rest, to make arrangements again. Rose Naismith ran into her husband more times than you would think if you were comparing their public (official) itineraries.

II

Parsley

Joan had a feeling about Parsley from the beginning. From the moment Stone's need-to-know notes arrived in the middle of the night, telex bells ringing to rouse her from sleep.

> CODE-NAME PARSLEY, BECAUSE
> SHE'S GREEN BUT GOOD. WENT IN
> AND OUT OF PARAGUAY, NAIVE,
> WITHOUT HELP. DAGMAR GOT ON
> TO HER QUITE BY CHANCE.
> THE NUNS HAD HEARD OF HER BUT
> HAD NEVER SEEN HER.
> THEY RANG THROUGH TO DAGMAR
> AT HQ AND WE FLEW OUT TO SEE
> FOR OURSELVES.
> PUT HER STRAIGHT INTO THE FIELD
> TRAINING IN PEKING
> THEN OPERATIONAL IN THE
> COLONY.
> LATER WE WILL PUT THE TASK TO
> HER.
> SHE'S AUS, WHICH SHOULD SUIT YOU.
> HOPE YOU ARE RIGHT ABOUT THAT
> LACK OF HISTORY.
> I'LL BE IN LONDON TO SET UP THE
> CONNECTIONS NEXT WEEK AND
> THEN IT'S PARIS IF ALL GOES WELL.
> DAGMAR WILL DO THE TALKING AS
> YOU SUGGESTED THEN IT'S ON TO
> THE BIG A FOR ME. STONE.

12

A criss-cross of plots and plans

A criss-cross of plots and plans
counterplots and sleights of hand
a cast of discreet cliques and networks
combine
these mutual strangers and mutual suspects
might have much in common.

Joan and Amelia had been holidaying at Guerella Beach since 1956.

They might have agreed, said
It's going to be a good summer.
Without pressure.
Sinking into the sand. The hours of driving done.
The days of the year over.
Obliterated from on-holiday minds.
The night silence.
The lurid obvious symbolic dreams.
The sea.

Rituals and habits.
They are deceptive.
Make up stories to explain the large transgressions.
Global fiction(s)
Mirrors the parochial, the personal.

There is an absence of innocence.
The air feels like the devil.
Like knowledge.
This is a summer warm and thick with plots and intimations.
Holidays stretch limits and fantasies.
Relationships might snap with proximity.

Guerella Bay. 1979-80. An all but private beach resort. Discreet houses in natural bush that runs onto the sand. No shops. No phone. No riff-raff. Car access only, and isolated beaches, walking tracks. Rocks islands caves forests of spotted gums maidenhair moss currawongs magpies kookaburras little black snakes and large goannas a hawk with a five-foot wing-span rides the air over two inlets and up into the third headland. You can watch it and the horizon seven miles out, then beyond, the Tasman Sea, the date line, the Pacific Ocean.

The cliffs and hills cut out the sun before it sets (this is the east coast of Australia) giving an indistinct end to everyday, an evening air of uncertainty. It is dark in the shacks and houses while the islands and rocks off shore turn pink and purple at whim, then silver, then steel.

And who is here?

Edith and Cecil. Two bourgeois romantics with appropriate props in this ancient landscape — bottles of excellent red wine, avocados, strawberries, silk shirts, Italian sandals. They are secure and incongruous.

Edith alone in the beach house at night would turn off all the lights and turn the music up loud and sing and dance. Eerie. Losing herself. Then she slept soundly.

Cecil wondered how she slept so well. As if nothing were ever on her mind. Like a clock. No, a computer. He described her so, though his poet's mind had to squirm to make those metaphors. So technical. So crisp. And so unlike his voluptuous wife. Such dissonance. It made him smile.

Cecil often tired of being the poet, the major poet. Even that did not always please. Acclaimed, secure, wealthy, a man of integrity, the view seemed to constrict, tunnel, go fuzzy at the edges and he could no longer see what or why.

He lectured less and less these days. The universities had grown larger and the cities dirtier. His collaborations and colleagues seemed anti-poetic and he could find nothing grand or moving in the young slash and shout phenomenon that turned up in his workshops. He thought it bad enough that they took themselves seriously, worse that they expected him to. And he had overheard. They had a nickname for him, P.C. Plod. Edith had to explain that they regarded the literary establishment as moral cops, class censors. Where did she get such knowledge/language? It was most disturbing of one's sleep.

'I dreamed I was playing the final at Wimbledon. The last few shots and game-set-and-match. The umpire breathed deep and said, "Cecil Evans has won the war." And I looked at the crowd cheering, smiling faces next to dead and mangled bodies, anguished faces,' Cecil blurted to Edith over breakfast. 'Oh, you poor darling. You have altogether too much social conscience. You know Dr May said that white middle-class guilt is a disease just like leprosy.'

By the following morning Cecil was dreaming safely, smilingly, of girls in wild-west taverns and he coming to the end of a long ride. Cecil was ready to be contacted.

Irving Stone. Back from the shuttle, Panama City, Miami and back down the coast to Acapulco. He worked a circuit. Became a familiar. These things took time. Setting up. Waiting to jump on and off the merry-go-round. Now he is strolling from the bush down to the beach, striding in the long evening, drinking a small social beer with the men at the boats on Rosedale Beach, after gentle fishing in the calmer waters behind the islands and the headlands. This time he is a chap called Clive, Edith's housekeeper, do you mind!

Howard H. Howard. Born 1926. Moved to Australia from Washington some time in the second half of the sixties. He burrowed into upper middle-class suburbia with an energy and delight that wasn't all fake. Agnes Smythe-Howard called her husband 'Tip', not because he was messy around the house, which he was, but because what you saw of him was just the tip of the iceberg. This was a private joke she took with her when she left him and Australia back in 1972, the same year Howard, apparently ill and with his hair turning quite white at the age of forty-five, retired to live permanently on the south coast. That was in May. A bitter cold winter that year. A good climate for icebergs and cold-blooded thinking. Howard had his moment (all anonymous of course) in 1975.

Elsewhere, but not in this novel, which does not go in for histrionics or conspiracy theories, Howard is known as Mr X. Here at Guerella Beach he wears a red track-suit, doesn't smoke, walks instead with his hands clasped behind his back. His hair is thick and white, a natural development that made it possible for this Third Under-Secretary of the oil-buying arm of the Defence Department to retire early and without suspicion. He lives in a solid brick house, wooden beams, big windows. His views of beaches and islands are close but largely symbolic. Howard no longer needs to observe the signals and struggles of smugglers' boats loaded with dope and desperados. The business is clean now. His information comes by word of mouth and his orders go out the same way. The operation is large and stable, entrenched, its dues are paid up well in advance (they'll be running a superannuation scheme next!). Howard uses couriers, the trusted, they talk openly, expound and explore the 'company' policy. CIA? And Howard leaves the nuts and bolts, the shit and piss, the blood and vomit, the eating and sleeping and boredom and repetition to the minions.

It was Howard who briefed the Stanleys on their posting to Australia and it was he who suggested Cecil (from an extensive short list) as a likely stooge. But it wasn't he who saw that Cecil's naivety could be used to play the pawn in another game. It would be tricky. A risk. But such a nice touch. So the four minds played it for a perfect coup de grâce...

(A formally histrionic paragraph)
Like Cecil, Howard was a dealer in metaphor and simile, in rhythm and time, in making moments all, captive. Like Cecil, Howard made words into a specialised sort of sense and sent them out into the world to make their effect through an exclusive set of receivers, a network of ears, privileged, an audience, a cast of players who took the world as their stage. Howard, like Cecil, had big ideas. Howard, unlike Cecil, carried a gun.

Gloria and Roy Stanley. It was Howard who brought the new couple to the all-but exclusive bay. And because it was Howard there were no questions asked, not even unspoken ones, though there was comment of the rhetorical kind couples address to each other last thing before they roll over to read another chapter of the latest Len Deighton.

'I hear she has money of her own,' Betty Baxter found herself saying to Bob over breakfast the next morning. Bob was reading the weather map with an ear on the radio to pick up the local fishing information through the static.

There were limits, Bob had decided, to getting away from it all. Betty liked the quiet, the rituals, of plain bush living by the sea. The house had been her mother's, built by an uncle in the thirties. The living had been much harder then. 'Or much the same,' remarked Bob lightly, careful not to carp as he sawed wood for the water heater.

To get out of Canberra in mid-summer, anywhere out of Canberra, was, for a few days, a fortnight even, bliss. By the third or fourth week Bob Baxter ached for a bit of slash and fast action, the word, the story, the story behind the story, the undercover cover, the mild realities that lay behind Len Deighton's popular fictions.

Bob Baxter had always liked the Yanks (or the marines as he called them when there was work to be done). He was comfortable with clichés, status quos, soap operas and eyes on main chances. Gloria Stanley seemed to be offering, that was enough of Hollywood in this rustic holiday community to give Bob Baxter his first decent sleep for a week.

Bob Baxter. Canberra Press Gallery. Undercover ASIO. Subterranean MI5 (or was it KGB? it was hard to tell the difference). He knew the CIA employed women. More and more of them in these modern times. There were forty field officers in Australia, mainly in training. Gloria Stanley was one of them though she worked only occasionally, for pleasure perhaps, or because she had, as Betty Baxter knew, money of her own. No. Because she believed. That only the intelligence services could keep order. And she might have believed it passionately.

Joan Stevens and Amelia Seine left for Guerella Beach on Christmas eve. They arrived at ten that night and unpacked the car in the bright moonlight. The house sat dry and the same as usual, leaves caught in the spouting, strings of bark blown up onto the verandah. They opened all the windows and lit a fire inside and made tea which they took down to the beach, to watch the stars and the silence and the sea after the pressure of the last few weeks. Joan and Amelia turned their backs on the hills and bush, tomorrow they would notice who was here and who was talking to whom, but tonight they had simply arrived at the end of a long drive and, spies or no spies, they were going to rest. The breeze came off the sea and cleared their heads.

Like all Christmas days that have ever been this one was unpredictable and did not go as planned. The weather was abominable. The rain began at dawn and kept up until late afternoon. It was impossible to step off the verandah without slipping in the clay. Joan headed off up the surf beach in runners and Japara over shorts. Howard was fishing off the surf beach with the determination of ritual. The sea was boiling and any fish he hooked would be a fluke. They greeted each other with familiar waves and nods, 'G'day', close up, 'Bugger of a day'. Joan climbed the steps cut into the clay bank and headed for the bush across the headland. The track to the lighthouse was deserted, Christmas dinners were being consumed in a few million houses, exotic drinks and rich food, family arguments and sleeping in the afternoon — a funny sort of ritual but not unpleasant, for one day of each year.

Joan read the old and new graffiti in the bunker left from the Second World War. She copied some apparently Arabic or Japanese glyphs on to the back of a supermarket receipt and went on to the end of the headland and looked up and down the coast at the wall of water pouring from the sky, no horizon, no clear sky in the south, and the rest of the continent in the third year of drought.

She sheltered under an overhang and studied the supermarket receipt. She wrote the decoded message in the dirt and read it several times over, sent the paper to the rain and wind and headed back the way she had come, stopping to watch a bird caught wet and unable to fly in a banksia tree. Could she help? No. Frighten it to death more like it. She rubbed the marks from the concrete wall of the bunker and walked along the wet clay roads to the house, noting cars and chimney smoke as she went. The weather was good for some things.

Amelia and Stone were well into their second scotch when Joan arrived at the house dry from the knees up. Stone greeted her with immediate talk, as if they were continuing a conversation recently interrupted. They had not met before. This first meeting was unscheduled but Stone, with the mobility and disguise of Edith's home-help, had made some astonishing discoveries and would rather have bailed out of the whole thing. It was all right for them. They melted into the scenery, were part of the familiar scheme, he was in from the outside and playing a role not entirely comfortable to a man in possession of certain scruples. 'Besides,' he turned to Amelia and demanded, 'how much do you actually know about what goes on down here? I mean, you put it together all right and I know you're acquainted with these characters socially and by their reputations but honestly, I think you might be out of your depth. This is the big league. Slick. Many ropes knotted tightly together to a particular purpose.'

'Yes. We know,' Amelia spoke. 'You have done fairly well to see that so quickly. No one is here for no reason. We are playing a long shot and it isn't vital that we bring it off, but it's the very front-line nature of this crew here that makes us think we have to try. We have to be able to operate on this level.'

'Besides. You're in there, aren't you? I got your message from the bunker. You're clear in there, and you can leave on Monday if you want to.'

Stone sighed and acquiesced, 'OK. Right. But you know I had a close call with Naismith in Canberra and he's due here in January. I'll have to be gone by then, even so it's a risk, what if he decides to pop down for the weekend?'

'Having trouble keeping so low, Irving? Just one more week and then it's back to the bright lights for you, OK?'

'OK'

It was Stone's contention that the Canberran Baxter and the 'Australian' Howard and the American Stanleys were cooking up several things over their obligatory barbecues on the lawns of the large house overlooking Rosedale Beach two bays up from Guerella. Stone noted the proximity of Stuart from the southern press and Bruggs from the NSW Right. It was a peculiar combination and no amount of on-holidays-forget-our-rivalries-stuff would convince him otherwise. He supplied full lists of names and left Joan and Amelia to put the pieces together.

It was Gloria Stanley they followed that blistering Boxing Day as the sun, having come out at last, proceeded to steam the countryside for a few hours and then simply blasted it with brightness, the rainstorm a memory; tomorrow there would be a total fire ban and the day after they would be complaining.

13

The poet had written the complete seascape

The poet had written the complete seascape — as he did every year — for declaiming at the stroke of midnight on the summer solstice. He would practise it the night before. A performance without an audience. An orchestral accompaniment of tinkling surf. Cecil declaimed to the stars and the sleeping seagulls. Naivety is not without its integrity.

Cecil thinks. This evening, this night before the summer solstice, all is imminent. Sinister omens and portents are rallying. The rocks are a grey blur, then black shadow. The sea is steel. Cecil is imagining a plethora of war images. His legs shake with the excess of adrenalin. Today a piece of the puzzle fell into place. All those familiar but unrecognised faces, the unanswered telephone, the opened mail, the questions out of the blue from people he barely knew, the feeling that things had been gone through, rifled. For a long while he suspected Edith and contemplated divorce when suspicion was confirmed by her habits of duplicity. But Cecil was not comfortable as a paranoid (or as unmarried). His line of work required ambition. Clarity of purpose. An arrogance. And besides, he liked being married to Edith. She was good for his fiction. So Cecil was actually relieved when Gloria Stanley found him quite alone at Tranquil Bay and smiled, 'Ah. Now. Cecil, I have something rather serious I want to discuss. I sometimes do work for the...well... shall we say CIA... and I was wondering, that is, we have discussed whether you might...'

Cecil was puzzled all over again by the approach. He had no access to state secrets or even subversives. As a matter of taste rather than politics he avoided radical students and could only imagine that perhaps, with his command of language (a skill at cryptic crosswords) they might want him for decoding, if that was still a human task in these technological times. Furthermore Cecil had a red face and yellowish hair, hardly subtle or grey or shadowy, and Gloria had laughed at him imagining that he might tail a spot through downtown Melbourne. She hadn't actually asked him to do anything except be ready. Certain places at certain times. Paris/ Rome/New York if necessary. Cecil decided to accept. It would make good copy. He reserved the illusion that he could control his own life. Cecil was still a poet.

Here are two women walking the beaches and headlands. They are old fashioned of face and demeanour, red and blue shorts, white shirts, straw hats, lipstick. They carry handbags, wear sensible sandals. Their presentation is ordinary, not too obviously I hope, for this is Joan and Amelia, permanent fixtures of this summer landscape, they hope to go unnoticed by the sex-and-intrigue league. They noted.

It is a golden day at Guerella Beach. The sun is gold. White gold. What would be the relentless Australian sun if you weren't on the four week annual and it wasn't Janaury 1980. The letter came out of the blue sky. It dropped in a plane at Bateman's Bay and was waiting for him, Cecil, at the ranch where he was wont to go for a martini at five. The letter found him there, serene, slightly drunk and listening to the American talk.

An invitation. To attend the London Literary Society. March 1982. The code words were there. The location slightly disappointing. Edith would have preferred Paris or Rome. But all that aside, Cecil was pleased to accept.

Joan and Amelia drift along the tracks. Birds fly up before the brightness of their clothes. Their faces show distraction, the regular number of features. Joan has a wide mouth. Her hair is pulled back from her forehead. Amelia has prominent eyes, a beaked nose. Together or alone they drift along the tracks through the forests on the headlands. Coming down to beaches they swim and continue their journey, rarely stopping to sit and look. It would appear their pleasure is in the mileage, heads held high to catch the birds, the sky. It is as if they are not watching who goes where, who talks openly or covertly, who fishes in which boat and who, of the women, turn their heads to note.

They have noticed how Gloria Stanley meets her new lover Bob Baxter in secret and Howard's hand on Roy Stanley's shoulder and that Cecil is behaving exactly as expected.

In the long afternoons the women sit at tables detailing maps, checking names and pseudonyms, exchange rates and movements in the futures market. This is the hack work. The nitty gritty. The underpinning of the major moves. Outside they stoke a fire for the evening and make tea. Their conversation is strewn with the cryptic and the urbane. Matter-of-factly they plan the strategies of subversion, and then the details. They are aspiring to clockwork. They practise accounting and prediction on the tourists, the holiday-makers, the innocent bystanders as well as the swarms and surges of Canberra public servants, academics, diplomats and cynics, who pretend for the summer that they are not each and all merely props, or agents of influence.

The random factors need to be calculated, placed and timed. The secret undermining of the world power milieu shall be as much a matter of chance as determinism. They have grasped the ambiguity: plotting power and corruption in such a perfectly beautiful place.

By the end of this summer they believed they were done. Each aim and action plotted, each operative slotted into cover, each instruction issued, each fall-back and counter-ploy described and sent out along the air waves and postal routes of this convenient world. They believed their work was done. Now. Sit back. Monitor. Watch. Wait. They dismantled their connections, erased traces of their friendship, cried a little at their conclusions and opened a bottle of champagne.

Joan and Amelia, drunk and still drinking, loll in chairs and laugh — the laughter that tries to conjure up courage, that is also triumphant. They drink a toast. To those who have nothing to lose. No. To success. They sober. Drink strong coffee. Run through the steps again. The plan is set in motion. Many things could happen. They begin again the lists and notes that are the theorist's make-work. The night passes without their sleeping. They drink more coffee before they set off. Separate. From now on they are strangers.

14

Dealing with death

Mary Stevens is in Hong Kong dealing with a man with power cool eyes. She is to execute him. Kill him with her own devices. He is Crane. A king of sorts in the kingdom of crime. He runs a show with an army of defenders, a hierarchy of pretenders to the throne. His links with China are as infiltrator, capitalist mover, messenger, black marketeer. He deals in food and luxury goods, as well as drugs and strategic secrets. He has direct lines to the unchanging bureaucrats. For many years Crane has been known, ignored, tolerated and allowed to operate, a subverter of communism, his motives impure but useful, as are his methods. As American foreign policy shifts, concern about his operation grows. His armies and his existence become a threat. His subversion ranges in wider circles. A senator's son dies from an overdose of heroin supplied to the New York scene by one of Crane's many lines. Now only the Russians could find him useful and they are not interested, or so careless.

Mary Stevens had been Crane's guest at times during her stay in China. Through his contacts she survived two months of illegal residence. She was his guest now at the Hong Kong races.

In China Mary Stevens had lived a rigorous life. No alcohol. No drugs. She played a game of fitness learned even from the corrupt army officials and the so-called decadent women of tough reaction. She studied and practised through the long boring hours of briefings about essential military installations and the secrets of imperialist intentions. She learned meditation and all the mysterious body workings of super strength and resistance. She would need them. In Acapulco she had been told: Do what you are told in China. It is a preparation for another larger task. Crane is your protector there, thinks you are CIA. The CIA think you are CIA. When you are freed from that sort of imprisonment you will be Crane's guest. Tell him all you see and learn, every and anything. Be tough and competent. Be impressive. He might not want to sleep with you. Crane is an interesting man, heterosexual but not rampant, and quite mistrustful. He might respect you. Or find you unattractive. Eat well. Drink little. Sleep regular hours. You will need a sort of strength that cannot be got from indulgence. We promise you a real rest when this is over.

Now. You will be a guest in his fortress and will have opportunities to kill him there but you will be watched and searched and if you do it there it will be nearly impossible for you to escape. We will be able to set up a drop for you. A place to locate a weapon. You will have to chose a time and location and notify us and be exactly able to be picked up and gotten away.

Mary Stevens went over all this at the races while pretending to study the horses in the form guide. If Crane would seduce her, she could exploit the deadly implications of privacy. That had not happened. He had been a charmingly respectful host, effusive in his admiration and attention. He was carefully supportive, paying her off for the China job, it had served his interests dramatically and he had rewarded her with long graceful dinners, two or three guests with impeccable manners and unchallengeable honesty. Mary had enjoyed these feasts, the genteel storytelling which personalised power.

There had been private showings of good films and performances by the ballet, as well as the Melbourne Symphony Orchestra, one of the best in that part of the world. Mary was slightly thrown by this reminder of home but believed she had carried herself with international if not aristocratic dignity. There had been an evening at a private club where Mary had slipped her champagne into the flower vase and danced quietly with an assortment of sleek and heavily mannered men. By day she swam countless lengths of Crane's pool or lay soaking in the humid sunlight. She slept in the afternoons and rose in the very early hours of each morning to practise yoga exercises and thinking. No plan formed itself. This job was not going to be easy. Crane could leave Hong Kong at any time or decide her holiday was over. She would have to take some risk, make a plan and begin to carry it out, that was as far as she could see, she counted on the momentum of beginning to see her through to the brutal conclusion. She did not think of that.

An activity was needed. A start to the process. Shopping. A shopping expedition. An obvious way to begin in Hong Kong, supermarket to the world. She tried out some scenarios: clothing, a tailor, Dagmar could be a saleswoman, the privacy (innocence) of a changing room. Or jewellery. Miniature guns changing hands and perhaps Crane would come and advise her on the quality of diamonds or the best price for gold. That sounded better. And both ploys would be needed. Failsafe.

Mary donned her secret-code-sign yellow boots red coat and bright blue scarf. It was a ridiculous outfit but the watchers would follow as she wandered the streets window-shopping with feigned interest. She removed the scarf in a clothing emporium and wandered into the haute couture department selecting frocks to try on. Dagmar hovered by the changing rooms with her armful of selections. They undressed side by side in shiny mirrored closets and emerged, changed, to ask each other what they thought. The small talk couched the large.

'I need something more daring, dangerous, something with a subtle but powerful action, to go with some beautiful emeralds I want to buy. I saw them this morning in Hay Street. My husband hasn't checked them yet but he will tomorrow. I want to have just the right thing to wear when I try them on.'

'Emeralds?' Dagmar queried. 'Do you think this colour is mundane enough? I need something smart but discreet. I think the dove-grey would suit the emeralds but have you considered investing in jade? There's a marvellous little place at the back of Mud Lane. Graeme Wong's. Small, an almost secreted place above a moneylender's. You might consider him. Jade goes so well with black or even blue or cream. It's best with cream and that silk outfit really suits your colouring.'

And so the deal was made. Mary acknowledged the instructions by buying the cream silk suit. Tonight she would invite Crane to advise on her choice of jewels, to attend his death. And that night another dinner party entertained them. She warily aired her plans to purchase jade and held her breath over the dessert as none of the assembled guests suggested other places or better sources. Crane enquired how she had come across this superior piece of information. Mary Stevens chose an enigmatic smile, 'I too have my sources.' It seemed to come off so she made her pitch. 'Impeccable sources but not a similarly informed taste. I was hoping someone would come with me and, well, prevent me from making a mistake. I adore jade and can imagine that is not the best measure in such a business. Crane, you would know about these things, or of someone who does. Perhaps you, Mr Phillips, you speak of diamonds and gold, perhaps you . . .' she leaned intimately as she spoke and caught Crane by his vanity. Of course he would go with her, why, they hadn't been around the city together, he would take her to Graeme's and to Ronald's and to the Thwaites' rooms, she could see some jade and perhaps some silver; he was, he said, a man of some taste in silk and artifacts, would she like it if he. . .

Mary danced a dainty step between gratitude and decisions. She accepted the invitations to see silver and asked about reputable dealers in Tang, figurines and vases, and so a day of pottery and highly priced jewellery was planned with ease. Mary sipped her cognac and the conversation turned to horses and breeding and she listened, all ears, for a good tip for future days, a spy's untaxed superannuation.

Graeme Wong's shop was indeed up a thin lane and a thinner stairway. Graeme was tall and big-boned. His room was spotless, carpeted and filled with tall glass cabinets and velvet-lined cases. There were no windows, two doors, one the entrance and another that lead to a private sale room, more luxurious fittings and secret soundproofing. It was to this room that Crane and Mary were led after Crane had suitably rejected the second-rate jade available for public inspection.

Dagmar was dressed in dull brown but smart as usual. Her hair was died black and pulled severely back. She wore glasses but no other jewellery. She sat at a small desk writing in a ledger. Her face showed no interest in their entrance. She stood and greeted them in French, a diverting touch, and walked away from the desk with its clutter of boxes and books. One box was set aside. She touched it as she went. This was Mary's sign.

Mr Wong entered and delivered instructions to Dagmar. 'Show Mr Crane the Shanghai collection, I will bring the Ming pieces from the safe which we can discuss over tea.' He disappeared through a door behind the curtain-wall as Dagmar began her work, a constant patter of history and information mixed with clues to style and quality. She set a large case on the display table and opened the one on her desk as she spoke. Mary caught her meaning and waited, looking at the pieces, fingering, holding them against her face, exclaiming at their coolness. She stood by the desk and examined the smaller case, a gun and some superb pieces. She removed the gun and carried the case to the centre table, hand and gun hidden beneath. She stepped up to Crane and levelled the open box at his stomach as if to show him, she raised it higher, aiming upwards, she pulled the trigger three times. Crane stared at her a second as the muffled pops crowded into his flesh. Mary stood very still staring at him. He died quickly, quietly, as if he'd been taught to die that way. Then she turned and followed Dagmar through the door behind the curtain.

It could be said that Mary Steven's first murder was easy, and yes, the act, the pull of the trigger one two three, and the crumpled soft body was, she decided, quite easy. But then the murder had happened over months, the death had been dealt slowly. From Acapulco and all through China Mary had chanted each minute, mute, I am going to kill a man. She used the rhythm of the words to regulate her breathing, to count off push-ups and leg stretches and the laps she swam in Crane's pool. When she decided, in Acapulco, to go with the Rocks and Stones of the world, I think she saw them as just another variety, engaged in the a-religious rituals of the corrupt. Her ambition was havoc, her ideology that of naivety, adventurism, anarchy — the danger and the prize. Mary Stevens too had embraced ambiguity.

Mary Stevens had not been convinced by grand idealism, by the vague resounding arguments for expropriation of western wealth for Third World survival. She was motiveless. An adventuress, and accepting. Partly she liked the prestige. Egotist. They wanted her. They believed she could do it. Insecure. Partly she didn't care about anything anyway and this was one way of seeing more of the world than an L.A. or New York bar or a Brixton squat or a hippie-ridden opium den in Thailand. She didn't mind not owning jade either.

So Mary Stevens dealt death on a close summer afternoon in Hong Kong and fled down thin stairways and through low-ceilinged rooms until at last, breathing deeply and clasping each other's arms, Mary and Dagmar stood safe in the garage deep underground. Mary felt tired, so tired. She sank into the black-windowed limousine and grabbed at a large bottle of scotch. She took huge draughts, was immediately drunk and had to be carried onto the small private jet. She vomited continuously across the Pacific

Ocean, regaining consciousness and sense as the plane made its descent over Vancouver. She reached again for the whisky and Dagmar had to hold her upright as she stumbled through the clear plastic airport and into the still clear night of a late Canadian summer.

Mary Stevens was comatose at the Mild Moose Lodge perched high on a saddle amidst tall pine trees and patches of semi-permanent snow. Dagmar was indulgent as Mary swung between unconsciousness and desperation. She lay still on a bed and slept and drank for four days until even she could not keep it up. On the fifth morning she burst out with brilliant energy, marching off up the mountain only to be dragged back drunk (from the medicinal flask) with frozen feet and bursting lungs.

Mary sank into a deep gloom as Dagmar pumped her with vitamin B and Stemital injections to stop her vomiting as well as tales of sordid intrigue and bloody death and her own training experiences. Mary was piqued. How could they be so uncaring? She had killed a man. Killed. Killed a man. Her body jerked as she chanted, her breathing regulating itself. She had an urge to do rhythmic exercises and finally floated off on this mantra into a web of mystical ignorance/resolution/peace.

Dagmar was delighted by this. She grasped the habit of this behaviour and fed it rice and tea, recreating the China rituals. Mary ate and drank and slipped in and out of her trance. Days passed. Weeks. Her Hong Kong suntan faded to wan whiteness. Her bones showed as angles, transparent. Her mind hibernated and forgot, put away into another time. She emerged very late one evening to demand chicken and peas and coffee and to sit with Dagmar (before an open fire), blazing, as they say, with an unnamed desire.

But such a tantalising interlude was not to be. Dagmar was at all times a worker. She stroked Mary's hair and rubbed her neck and shoulders with thoughtful vigour. They talked that night, or Mary did, constantly. Years of words poured out, or so it seemed, though if you had been listening, and certainly someone was, you would have heard the blandness and cliché of confessional talk that the re-establishment of identity seems to require. Yawn. Dagmar waited and massaged the iron bars of anxiety into sleepy silence. Mary slumbered, murmuring, reaching out a hand, a touch. Dagmar waited and left in the first light. Mary woke later, relaxed and warm, the fire still glowed, her packed bags standing in the corner. She put herself in the shower and into the present, flipped the destination tags on the suitcase handles and smiled. Paris. The place of culture and decadence, of radical politics and neurosis, of romance and artifice, of art and the unconscious. She sighed with relief. Paris would be her holiday (said the brief note from Dagmar) and the past just a dream. Love. Mary burnt the note in the last ember of the fire and waited for her life to be taken over one more time. A local man drove her down the mountains and through the neat suburbs of Vancouver to the airport. Sleeping tablets through the long flight above the edge of the polar cap and down to the earth of anciently civilised Europe. It felt like coming home.

15

A Fact. Some Notes. A Postcard.

A Fact
John Paisley, top CIA specialist on the Soviet Union, dead in Chesapeake Bay near Washington, 'his abandoned yacht contained highly classified communications gear capable of communicating via satellites linked to the CIA ground station at Pine Gap Australia'.
National Times, August 1980

Some Notes
Sometime before she forgot about it completely Mary Stevens made a series of notes in code which she posted to herself care of her mother's holiday house. It was an attempt to order and claim, for her own future, for herself if she ever needed it, the events and knowledge of the previous three years. It might be of use one day. A mind now so intent on denial might one day want to invoke.

Twenty pages in all she typed in the reading room of the library to be posted from various post offices as she came across them in her wanderings about Paris. The notes were cryptic but full and detailed, containing names, dates and places, quotes from Dagmar and Stone, descriptions of all she had seen in China and Hong Kong, the breeding histories of good horses, names of owners, trainers, connections. There were lists. Who she thought she could remember visiting Crane — Houghton, Hand, Naismith — or those mentioned in passing in the candid conversation over dinner. She raided her ravaged brain for the names and interconnections, cabinet ministers, department heads, French nuclear testers and safe houses, they might not hold for the future but she imagined if she looked at them long enough a pattern would emerge, a picture of reality far locked into an elitism that she was only beginning to understand.

Vancouver. December. 1980.

Dear Mother,

I know you do not worry about us, the long times between postcards. I just don't seem to get the time for letters, besides, we never have been correspondents. Back on the N. American continent briefly, I hope to recommence quickly a new job. P.R. Curralero's have a new job. P.R. Curralero's or I travelling, but I should be able to keep in more regular contact. I heard somewhere Lopez had died in Paraguay. I get the feeling it could have been true but the did it indeed it's frightening what a dictatorship of illegality to do to the inhabitants; and oppressed while making millions for the thugs and governments they pretend to be to outrages! I bet you'd pleased north this were if moralistic outrage. More later

Luv Perry.

MRS JOHN STEVENS
41 MOORE ST
FOOTSCRAY HEIGHTS
VIC. AUSTRALIA.

AIR MAIL

Canada 17
La Rose Montreal
Les Floralies de Montreal

The notes were random and chaotic, an eccentric code (a bit like this novel), but they might serve as triggers or switches, were better than nothing: some connection to the future Mary Stevens, one she was increasingly unable to contemplate. She addressed the envelope to herself care of the Malua Bay post office which was the nearest to Guerella Beach, the safe place, a safe house from childhood memory, rarely visited now. She imagined her mother would collect them and keep them for her and perhaps she would not open them and even if she did they would not make much sense, just another example of her strange daughter's distant and irrelevant life.

As she posted the last envelope she crossed her fingers. It was something done for herself. Wasn't it?

Summer, Southern Hemisphere. 1980-81

The talk at Guerella that year was all about the super-secret (written in invisible ink even) CIA study which told that from what they knew was turning up in Moscow the KGB had magnificent sources in Australia, they're getting a top product from somewhere. Howard was irritated. Everyone *knew* about the Russians. It was a concession. Part of the deal. The two codes had to intersect at some point. The Middle East was far too volatile. Likewise Africa, all sides had too many troops and arms. South America was not safe for any American, and that same Yank could not go behind the Iron Curtain, too many killed on that road. A small-time liberal democracy, controlled and accessible, polite, rather provincial and only occasionally capable of putting on what they thought was a gripping show. Australia. Strategically ideal. The Brits regarded it as a bolt-hole, buying up land *pour après l'holocaust*. The Yanks made it a playing field with their installation at North-West Cape, a telephone switchboard? or perhaps it's there to keep score.

They talked up the jokes and the stakes and it was agreed: no leaks to the press, no statements, no talk to each other. And now there was gossip, idle chatter made by over-imaginative journalists and bored (or ambitious) academics. It could be contained. These leaks would take years to achieve public veracity and by then the programme would be over, all the names and dates changed...

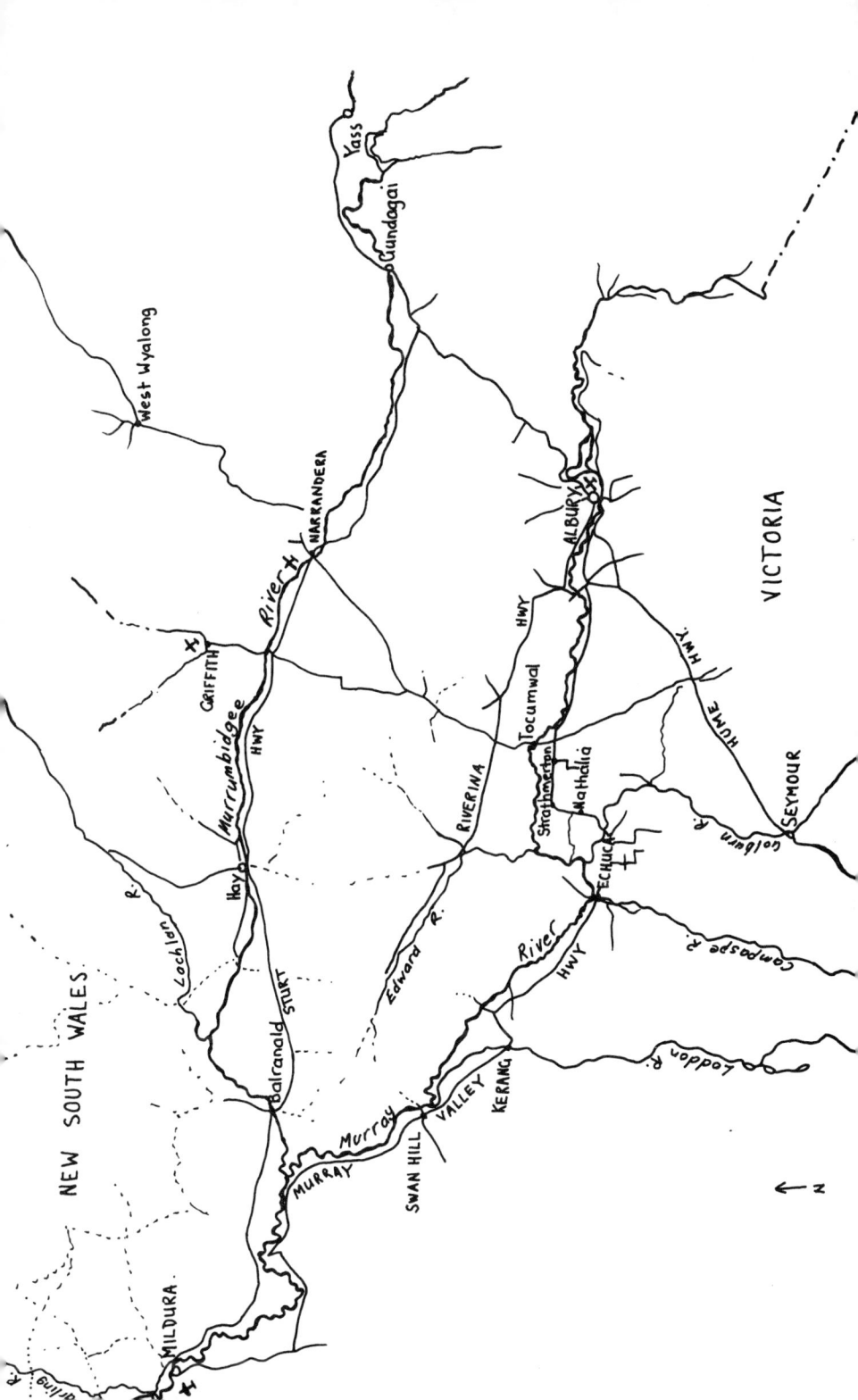

16

The plot (II). Mary Stevens in Paris

Mary Stevens spent five or six days touristing pleasantly about Paris. Waiting. Expectant. At a loose end. Nothing and nobody happened. Art filled her days as she traced the remembered streets of a hundred French novels; retracing her steps, she recalled two centuries of literature and politics.
Colette took her to more out of the way places, more intimate bars. Violette led her a merry dance through the famous back streets where Simone and Jean-Paul used to sip their strong blacks and comment, distanced, syrupy, on the passing parade of word-collectors. Colette laughed and bought an apéritif. Violette stared and stared and hesitated to ask them small questions. They seemed not to hear and then Jean-Paul turned his back and the women chatted, social prose. I bet Sartre eavesdropped, memorising their rhythms and lyric patterns (he would check through de Beauvoir's writing later, noting if it was accurate).
Mary Stevens stood in the Tuileries, the outdoor sculpture gallery, the Maillol women. She recalled an Australian friend whose famous photographer husband had brought her to these gardens to say, child-pleased with himself, look, there you are. Great sculpture and the women are like you are like them, short necks and thick ankles. There you are. As ugly or as beautiful as a Maillol woman.
Mary Stevens stood gazing, concentrating on seeing the greatness, urgent about appreciation. Does she know that she's behaving like the class she (unconsciously perhaps) has taken to hate?
She got off the metro at Stalingrad station, just because of its name, and was figuring the intricacies of traveller's cheques over a weak tea and butterless bread (the revenge of the French), when the man beside her spoke:
'Ah, you are a tourist. You are absorbed. These figures, they make no sense to you?'

Mary turned to piss him off, this slim dark man of indeterminate age, determined Frenchness, the accent. He continued speaking in English before she could arrange any words, 'May I help?' Mary stumbled into French 'Ah oui, je suis très...ah...no problem...' she gave up, said, 'It's OK, thank you,' and turned away.

Just how they asked each other if they would like a drink or how they proceeded to pass the perfunctory hours of courtship escaped Mary Stevens' memory entirely.

As well it might, for her waiting had ceased; someone had happened. Her luck, it seemed, had changed. Pierre was still there in the morning, dark curls above the sheets, glasses on the bedside table within reach. Mary pretended to be asleep as she tried to remember if she had done anything wrong or embarrassing or dangerous.

The sidewalk café was a hectic setting for breakfast after a hard night. Mary needed to walk, to find some activity that would keep this stroke of luck, this sexy Frenchman, from striding off into the realms of another one night stand. So she walked to the markets and practised with the currency and was sure, could have sworn, that was old Violette Le Duc buying tomatoes at the next stall.

It seemed (or would have, had you been watching) that for a few weeks Mary Stevens had found happiness where many people did, in autumn in Paris with a man named Pierre. Mary had been calm and a little smug with this delectable person and his delicious attentions, not to mention his predictable name. She allowed him to show her Paris, to wine and dine and drive her about, to go leisurely to bed with her and leave courteously before breakfast each day.

Soon she was overwhelmed by the constancy of his attention and, like any practical girl, or one in need of flattery, she started seeing things in terms of affection. Her diligent efforts at French seemed to take wing as she stumbled less and her accent improved. She even began to dream in French, albeit in black and white, like the few French films she had seen.

She and Pierre were as one, it would have seemed (had you been watching). They now desired coffee simultaneously, a walk and brandy by the river within moments of each other. They walked in step and slept in an unbroken curve (their eyelids would even slip open in sync).

One day, while walking by the river, they simultaneously noticed an apartment to let, with view. They went straight in and spoke courteously with the concierge who took their money and gave them the key. No shades of 'Last Tango in Paris' this, it looked for all the world like the first flings of permanency.

Mary moved from hotel to apartment that afternoon and she and Pierre shared a charming picnic of bread and fruit and cheese and wine on the bare floor with the sounds of street and river Seine as their atmosphere. They laughed at having to strain their necks out the bathroom window to see Notre-Dame way below and through the gap between the buildings. They went to bed early and murmured yes and more and is that so sort of mundane magic late into the night. The next day Pierre went out for brioche, fresh coffee and a saucepan to boil water and he returned to stay long after breakfast and lunch.

Mary Stevens spent the late afternoon alone in sublime lethargy. Life seemed to her (and she was watching) to be wonderful and perfect and surprisingly simple for a change. She wondered briefly why it had not always been like this but these days the past seemed so far away, like a foreign country, she mumbled, conveniently forgetting she had been at home like this in several foreign countries in the past few years.

It would have seemed, had anyone else been watching, that Mary Stevens had forgotten all she had learned in the Paraguayan jungle or atop the Chinese cupboard. (Of course there were several people watching.)

An extract from Mary Steven's diary, a slim volume she began to keep in Paris. There were entries for three weeks.

> Well. Pierre. Are these the first days of romance? Is this vagueness like those movie moments of glittering silences? I'm sure our eyes shine, hands touching across starched white tablecloth. Mary & Pierre. Me and him. Pierre is shortish, thin, with pale skin. Almost young and with that air of translucence that some men acquire, that some women admire. (Je t'adore.) I mainly admire his eyes, of course. Behind his glasses they are deep and dark and so full of passion, so full of restrained romance. I cannot help but sigh to my reflection in the mirror. Such eyes. One meets them rarely in these days of alcohol and defences, of battered hearts and everyone is so experienced, so bored with their desires. Stop. I don't like the tone of that.

17

Instant coffee

Moving from Paris is more complicated than moralism, and more dangerous.

The trail is hardly one for tourists though if you go along it you will see a sort of Australia that is neither city nor outback but the space and closeness of rural, agricultural, the settled.

You drive south from Colleambally and west to Hay. It's a long straight flat road with too many kangaroos feeding too close and risking it because of the drought. Blink and miss Balranald and cut across the dirt roads through low country to hit the Silver City Highway above Wentworth. Blink again and cross the Murray to Mildura. You will have to skirt the edges of this town, it has an eleven p.m. curfew, but drive along the river roads until you hit the Murray Valley Highway at Swan Hill. It's five a.m. and there are no roadhouses open. You sleep for an hour or two and get blustered awake by a semi racing into Kerang and there is even a half-quaint café though the coffee is instant. Cohuna. Then Echuca. Heading east through the rich irrigated land across the Campaspe and the Goulburn, it's a pretty drive. Turn left and hit the highway again, turn right near Nathalia and you head away from the river and the standing bush. Neat paddocks, irrigation channels, Katunga, Strathmerton, tiny towns hardly breathed in on Saturday afternoons in winter when the football is away and the little kids play on the sides of the roads, races are listened to, nuns have birthday parties, cakes are baked, trees climbed, you drive into town but want to keep on going out. So conspicuous. There is no preventing that. Best to go to the pub and have a beer. Someone will talk to you and you might find out who around here might know how Davidson is doing all right suddenly. The men in the bar look and stay silent but later they talk about the drought and the low prices for fruit and beef and how a man's gotta keep body and soul together and they put five more off at the factory and now it's autumn and some of the blokes would walk off tomorrow if they had a job to go to.

Fact: In 1981 the Riverina marijuana crop had an estimated value greater than the actual value of the Griffith grape crop.

18

The plot thickens

Mary Stevens didn't notice the Russian invasion of Afghanistan or the latest Nuclear Power Plant Failure or the fuss over the Moscow Olympic Games. No, that is not entirely true. She noticed them but paid no attention to such serialised pseudo-dramas. Mary and Pierre were much more preoccupied with the politics of their own relationship than with the comings and goings of Mishka and Ivanov.

What began as a perfectly straightforward affair was developing into something of an epic. (Everything is relative.) Mary Stevens had woken in her small apartment, a frown already formed on her brow. She knew that today she would have to think. There was no avoiding it. When she woke up frowning she knew she would have to devote many hours to sorting and resorting the recent past.

'Right. Let's go back to Saturday,' she said in a cheery voice to the view out the window. 'Pierre was leaning out that window just watching the street when I woke up. We talked. Something about him. That's right. Visits to the country. I remember feeling OK about that. Affirmed. It was conventional love affair chat. Then I asked him to help me with my French and we ended up going to bed and then to a bookstore and hearing some writers read, in French. They were quietly passionate and I picked up quite a lot of it but really, I thought at the time, a play or even a movie would be better for my purposes. (There are actions and expressions that give you clues.) I suggested a play but Pierre said he had something to do and that I should go by myself and that he would meet me in the café afterwards. He didn't quite say so but I got the impression that he didn't care for going out. I went to "Tartuffe" and didn't understand a lot more of the French but I felt OK sitting in the café ordering a Ricard. Pierre and I had been to this café several times so I was hardly even surprised when the barmaid spoke directly to me with a message from Pierre. He would be a little late she said he had said. I smiled and thanked her (in French) and she stayed to talk to me for some minutes.'

'Perhaps I did think all his telephone concern was apology, for not staying another night. Perhaps, but I think not. Or not consciously. And I certainly didn't think of it the next day because I slept until he came banging on the door with roses and champagne and chocolates, do you mind. It was all so extreme. I couldn't think of anything; I was laughing so much and having coffee and chocolates for breakfast feeling ridiculously corny. It was sunny and blue-skied and a quiet Sunday morning (and I was apparently being romanced by a delightful man). I might have believed nothing had changed.'

Extract from Mary Steven's diary. December 1981.

Pierre has gone to Versailles for few days with his 'sister' Ruth. I am again alone in Paris. Things have changed. I sit in this apartment, this room. The sun shines through the windows. I feel very isolated. I miss Pierre immediately. Persistently. He has gone to the country with his sister. They left last night. In Ruth's blue car.

The night before last we went to a restaurant where the waiters were as subtle as French sauces. We drank wine and ate several courses, slowly. It was as if we'd always been sitting in a restaurant, quietly, talking about our past, our future. I said I wanted to live somewhere permanent for a while. Some pretty coastal town where the sun shone and the tourists were bearable. (Why did I say this?) Pierre suggested a few places in Spain and Portugal and that night we lay together and built a cottage, our cottage, our leisurely days of intimate ritual. At the restaurant I had asked Pierre what work he did, how he lived. He told me stories of his family, amounting to a vague sort of fortune and several brothers and sisters. He said he never had to work and I was surprised when he told me he would be teaching a course in archaeology at the Sorbonne next term. (My source of income was never broached.)

Ruth arrived for lunch the next day, that is yesterday, and, now that I think about it, it is clear that they had arranged to go away together. Pierre took no luggage, or none from here anyway. I *still* do not know where he lives. Ruth has a large house so perhaps he lives there or has an apartment somewhere.

Ruth found me in the Café Noir today. She walked directly to my table and sat down. I assume she expected to see me. She had a message. From Pierre. He would be back in Paris tomorrow and we could go to the theatre and then to dinner. It was quite a formal message and made me feel silly for being so maudlin and obsessed with his absence. I have spent the last two days mooning and sleeping and walking in the parks, from the café to the river and home at three or four in the afternoon in order to have plenty of time to be depressed and lonely. I have written several letters. This is not at all like me and I must make an effort to stop. Ruth asked me to dinner at her place tonight and I accepted for something to do other than listen to Paris.

I had dinner with Ruth last night, there were several people there so I didn't have to talk much. I listened to two or three languages and got a little drunk. A man called Aaron spoke quite seriously to me about art and his country house. I listened and asked interested questions. I was drinking two glasses of wine to everyone else's one. Ruth and I are going shopping today. I keep getting regular cheques from the past and assume they will continue. After all, this is supposed to be my holiday. I shall spend my money while it comes.

I spent a lovely day shopping with Ruth and Angela. Of course, they know all the good places and all the helpful people. I bought some dresses and shirts and trousers. I saw a lovely grey coat but Ruth said it would look dowdy next year and that I ought to buy green. We had a sauna and a massage and lunch at a private club. I feel terrific today, the powers of consumption perhaps, though I'm sorry I didn't get the grey, I do not mind that Pierre is absent. Tonight I am going to Angela's for cocktails. Then we might go to the cinema.

Pierre is back. Not that I would know, but I swear I saw him at the club last night. Angela, Paul and I went there for coffee after the movies (I think they are quite well off) and I swear I saw Pierre at the bar but there was nothing I could politely do to make sure. When I managed to excuse myself and go to the toilet he was gone. I am confused but not too much so. Perhaps I'm a little crazy. I have had a nice time these last few days.

Angela came by for lunch today and asked if I would like to go to Rouen with them for the weekend. The cathedral is enticing. I am tempted but certain to decline. I rang Ruth as soon as Angela had gone and asked her if she'd seen Pierre. She was surprised or maybe a little cross. She said she had seen him for lunch and that she assumed he'd been in contact with me although they didn't talk about it (that is, me, of course).

I felt very low after that. She was all sugar and spice but I felt distinctly as though she was being rude. What did she mean 'They didn't talk about it'? Why not? Does she regard me as an embarrassment? Too lowly to be conversed about? And she was so charming (if a bit condescending) when we went shopping. Angela and Paul have been perfectly interested in me and my life. Even asked questions about Australia. I am very confused and feel a deep fear in the place where sweet reason normally resides.

I rang Pierre's office. Madame Anna said 'He's out and won't be back...' I wait. I sit in our apartment and watch the street from behind the lace curtains. I rush about and tidy things away. I make the bed and clean the toilet. I pack all my new clothes away. I take a bath and wash my hair and get dressed in the new clothes. I stop myself from going crazy. I sit behind the lace curtains and smoke cigarettes and watch the sky go dark. I am making myself go crazy.

I become obsessed with self-loathing, with self-pity, with recrimination. At eight o'clock I ring Pierre's office and listen for minutes to the dial tone. At ten past eight there is a knock on the door. I am paralysed. I have been so absorbed in the dial tone I have forgotten to listen for his footsteps. I wait a casual moment. I light a cigarette. I open the door. It is not Pierre.

19

Clandestiny

Mary Stevens gathered her shattered self-image into old black slacks, a sweater and put on a close-fitting cap. Right. You've marched out of Paraguay and slunk through China. Fled Hong Kong and wandered about Paris, been trained for subterfuge and insanity, now you have to go into action on your own life. She put on a pair of black runners, tucked her hair under the cap, took smokes and matches, 2000 francs in the back pocket, she slid into the brightly lit street, ducked down to the metro to glide across town to Ruth's place.

She left the train a stop early, a perfunctory precaution, and came to the house silently. Check. House lights on. Expectant air. She peered through the fence, slid open the gate, crept into the bushes, partly hidden. She crouched, waiting for regular breathing, a cigarette. The charade had started.

The house was lit upstairs and down, curtains drawn on downstairs windows. Mary Stevens climbed a plane-tree, could see through the window on the stairs, down over the lounge room drapes, just an inch or two but enough. Mary watched, still and listening. Ruth was upstairs dressing before dinner, making turns before an invisible mirror. Felice the maid came into the room and Ruth and she walked down the stairs talking, details of the meal perhaps. The slice of view shrank toward the back of the house. Distant chatter. Two voices. Three. Mary, impatient and perched, lit another cigarette. She could wait. She could fill the waiting with lists and facts, with uncomprehended evidence.

Minutes and minutes passed. The lounge room and the garden gate and Mary Stevens waited. A car pulled up. Engine off. Tempting. Door slam, two, three. Gate. Two men pass through, a woman. Mary recognised Pierre before he came into view, she saw him, the others blurred. A brief view of his face, silent, relaxed, then gone into the house. The heart in the tree raced (stopped, started, slowed, anti-climaxed). She had known Pierre was back. She had. All this tree-perching had done nothing but confirm. Her bones sank with hurt and despair. She stayed in the tree suspended between absurdity and purpose, left leg asleep. Her eyes locked to a slit of lounge room light that promised before dinner drinks and conversation.

Pierre's voice. And Ruth's.

She was not sure. It was familiar but. . . What was that? Pierre had sighed. She heard it almost telepathically. A remembered sound from their shared moments of deep satisfaction, their exhaustion. And now clear words. 'She will have to be told, immediately. I cannot continue to hide out in my own city. I do not care for this cruel deception any more. My job is over. Yours must begin.'

Mary Stevens filed words rapidly, turning schizophrenic in order to hear the woman's reply. 'Is she all right? Does anyone know? Ruth? Angela? Why have you left her alone? We must know what she is doing at all times. Be sure she is not destroyed, made useless after all.'

Mary's ears popped with disbelief. Neck clenched, aching, anguished. That was Dagmar's voice. The night swayed about her and she imagined she had leapt from the branches, had crashed through the window, but Pierre was tense, gulping his drink, he scratched his forehead. Mary Stevens was suddenly telepathic and televisual. She could see every detail of the scene as if she had dreamed it the night before. Her gut-wrenching astonishment was that of a person who walks awake through a forgotten nightmare.

Ruth entered the room with a plate of food and an impatient voice, 'Why are you all so sensitive all of a sudden?' She said, 'You knew from the beginning how it would be. And you Pierre. This ridiculous concern, this vanity, and ego. All that rigid fortitude you've been wailing at me about. Objectification! That's what you said, of yourself, of course, not her. You get well paid for a few weeks of deadened emotions. And you Dagmar. My God. You've done worse to your own daughter. Phone her. Get her over here. Forget this trifling incident. Get it over with. We have work to do. . . Another drink?'

Mary Stevens slept that night at the Paris Royale and the next at the Ritz. Attired in the style of an English librarian she settled over a pot of tea in the salon. This afternoon's task: revenge.

Mary chose a public place, the club of course, respectable and careful of its reputation. Surely they would not kidnap her there. She phoned Ruth's house. Felice answered. Mary read a prepared statement through twice, as with a press statement, so Felice could get the details down without getting a word in:

> This is Mary Stevens. Stop. Tell Pierre to meet me at the Club at 21 hours and to reserve a table. Stop. Hungry. Stop.

She hung up and left the hotel immediately. Another taxi, another hotel, her trail was definitely there but she would keep going and hold on to hope (the optimist again).

At seven Mary dressed, black cat burglar outfit, covered with bulky coat. She spent two hours at the coiffeur next door to the club, being washed and permed, facialed and manicured. She left by the back door, crossed the yard into the club car-park. Easy so far. She spent ten minutes in the powder room waiting for that telepathy to give her a cue to move. She hung her coat in the hall and gently materialised on a stool next to Pierre. He had watched the front door for her entrance.

Was he confused? He looked mildly fed up. She fixed him with a hurt and angry gaze. He frowned.
'Where have you been?'
She mimicked his expression and sentence.
'Where have you been? Two whiskies please. No ice.'
'I'm sorry. It's all over between us. I've been away. Retreating from telling you.'
'You must explain,' she said calmly, deceptively unmoved but imperative. The drinks arrived. 'You must tell me what happened.' She sipped. 'We were so in love, so happy, so. . .' Tears, quite real, crept from her steely gaze. The tears did a neat job. Pierre squirmed, quite obviously, and reached for her arm. She almost couldn't bear to go on but he sputtered apologies and lies which solidified her resolve. 'I'm starved. Let's eat,' she said, 'we can talk over dinner. This will take a while.'

He finished his drink and followed her into the dining room. Seated she ordered champagne, 'Why not, maybe we're celebrating something.' Pierre regained wariness, 'Tell me where you have been? I have been frantic searching for you.'

'For two days only,' she said, 'That's how long I've been gone. But that doesn't matter. You were saying how sorry you were, perhaps you could tell me the whole story. Now.' She made serious swoops at the truffles as Pierre began.

'Well. I will tell you the truth. I will be plain and cruel. Perhaps it is better. I was hired to seduce you. It was a necessary step, to cover you. After Hong Kong you became visible, a target. (Some called you heroine, others, enemy number one.) No one could protect you twenty-four-hours a day, jail you with bodyguards or hide you out for years. That would be too expensive, Mary. You were trained for a reason. There is more for you to do. And you need a cover.' The salad arrived. 'What better than a cover blown. A woman in love and then wronged. Betrayed. You can see what that sort of emotionalism means. This is not the behaviour of an effective spy.' His words were almost lost in his eating. 'You can see how it has to be convincing. Can't you? Even now we are being watched from several sides.'

'But you liked me, didn't you? It wasn't all a game. You can't lie (laughing or) in bed. You can't. Or can you? Did you? I feel such a fool.' The champagne arrived. The waiter poured a spoonful into Pierre's glass, waiting for him to taste it. She picked it out of his hands, downed it, said 'Fine' to the waiter and 'Another bottle after this, if you please.'

Pierre made a cruel silence, took toughness from her just being there. 'Yes. There is no room for romanticism here. In bed I might think of money or ideology or pornography, many people are like that, even with the woman they love, and in the mornings I make regret into romance, stylish breakfasts.'

He turned grey and gritty in the refined dining room. Mary Stevens closed her eyes and clung to her fork, stabbed his hand through to the bone. She had hurt him and drawn blood but he maintained composure. She wiggled the fork free and signalled the waiter, 'Could I have another set please?' She sat back and gulped champagne, enjoying the crisp spatchcock and his inescapable pain.

The buzz of conversation in the dining room rose a fraction to drown Pierre's common cursing. Mary gulped another glass and attacked the plate of fish before her. 'I might kill you,' she said, 'or cut where it hurts most. How did you. . .' she piped, near hysteria at her own actions, the lack of control. 'How did you think it would work? I have been violated, raped by your hatred and contempt, and theirs.' That was too much to contemplate. 'Misogyny is too mild a word.' (And misandry too simplistic a response.) 'You have committed worse than murder against my flesh. You have betrayed yourself and your own desires, and mine, my god, you have assaulted my history, my psyche, you have made yourself a weapon, you are vile vile vile.' Her voice climbed higher above the discretion of the shimmering room. Argument and rhetoric were a waste of time. Mary Stevens sank into hysterical silence.

Pierre snorted. 'Fine. Very well played. Good. You will do. And damn you. How dare you! It's all very well. I get to take the shitwork, am allowed the bits and pieces while you sit there and whine about your precious sensibilities. Don't you realise, you're an operative, you get the exciting work, the big stuff, and I. . . I'm. . .'

Words failed both of them. Mary groaned, her heart, her head, she squeaked ridiculously, her knees clenched, she wished she were anywhere else. The champagne popped her catatonia, she reached for a tasty cigarette, drank the sparkling liquid at a draught, her head cleared, she had maybe five minutes before her blood stream overloaded with alcohol to end the immediate misery, make unconsciousness a careless solution.

She fixed Pierre with a sorry stare. 'OK. Now I say "I give up". Then I say "What do I do now?" What do you say?'

Pierre curled into a curve of regained power and relaxed. For him the worst was over.

Mary Stevens passed out.

20

The plot thins

They took Mary Stevens from the club, barely conscious and shaking with silence, to a room high in a large house where, while the sun shone through all the windows, the doors were a long way away and the stairs downwards invisible. Mary was kept there, or stayed there, she could not tell the difference. Sometimes she was angry prisoner, resistant brain-washed victim, at other times she was passive, the acquiescent agent or broken woman. The choice was hers, though no one knew.

In any pose she was consistent about one thing, she would no longer comply. 'This' she mumbles, 'is the end. But I will not give them my pride, my what-ever-it-is that might just keep me worth being alive.'

The room at the top of the house is flooded with sun-warmth and sunlight, there is stillness above street noise. Mary huddles on the couch or sits by a small diamond-shaped window fantasising about the days when it will be possible to journey simultaneously through time and space.

'Each day at midday one or two of us come to talk her round, to sound sweet promises of power and wealth and good deeds and time to make hay or sunshine or pearls of wisdom. With Ruth, Mary is angry, silent and set with fury. With Paul and Dagmar she is vague with disappointment, somewhere else. Depression drives her now, feeds her, she explores its endless circles, keeps finding new muscle to its strength.

Mary develops headaches and we must give her painkillers and sleeping pills, mere nurses to her patient anger.

She no longer bothers to speak the negative, to say no, won't do it, won't go on your fanciful missions that are never quite clear. . .

Eventually we bring her other faces, other voices to talk larger stakes, describe in detail the higher motives. These are mostly men Mary notices and giggles, stupid, crude, do we really expect her to be capable of trust or commonsense.'

Eventually the sameness of the days tell their tale of failure and refusal. Mary is abandoned. The late night talks of controlled power and implied violence become a dribble of weary optimism, it is clear they have ceased. The coffee is finally gone, the bread rock hard. She is alone and just alone. The sun still comes each dawn. The water is still hot in the bath but the doors stay closed and the days are endless in their boredom. Mary Stevens is disappointed, whipping neglect into another hungry sort of anger. She pulls clothes about her and strides down the unfamiliar hallway. The doors are open, slack and disinterested. The stairway is ordinary, unthreatening. Mary clumps noisily down through the empty house and flips open the front door. The street is there. Mary steps into the drift, walking, walking, physical exhaustion (the everywoman cure for confusion). She walks the street with a strong and purposeful stride, going nowhere fast, no memory, no present.

Mary Steven's Teacup

Mary Stevens popped into Madame Marie's to have a cup of tea and to have the leaves read. It showed:

Someone dancing on a pile of rubbish.
Someone who has lost their head (literally)
ranting with a big stick (quite sensible).
A steady line of talk and problems stretching
from the present to the future. (Oh shit)
At one side and close, a witch, a crone
stirring a concoction. (I don't need this.)
Not unfriendly
or making fear.

This cost thirty francs.

21

One night stand

Mary Stevens lay rigid, determined — I will not wake up. It's too early. I will not wake up and face (the awful memories), this day of regret and recrimination stretching empty before me. I will sleep. Sleep. Sleep through the headache (and the hideous self-hate). I will lie here. I won't move. I won't open my eyes. Non. No. Oh. . . bugger it. Her eyes opened. She stared at the ceiling just lit by dawn. Fuck it. It's so bloody early. It's dawn and I'm wide awake again.

Mary staggered defeated to the toilet, the tap, water, large gulps of water, miracle cure for hangover when taken with a handful of painkillers and speed. She lay back on top of the bed clothes and smiled, the memory of the last thirty-six hours, she laughed, congratulatory, there is much to be said for sex and the sordid. Huh! And who are you to moralise?

Oh Mary felt ashamed, a little, enough to have given the men false names. And it wasn't that they might know her again, or that she would ever see them again. It was the form required by the determination to go out and pick up a man in a bar, get roaring drunk (and enjoying that quite a lot) in order to fuel her false courage and sustain excitement through wild night life and into bed somewhere, then more drinking, another bed another man. Her shame began at the end of her orgasm and she lay back drinking and smoking, waiting for this one to get off, go to sleep. She scuttled from the bed and out into the streets. The sun had risen hours ago. She had missed the romance of dawn. The Paris streets were full of grey glare and hurrying to work faces and shoes. She slumped home to wash herself over and over again, going through a routine of washing soaping rinsing until exhaustion and grand boredom allowed her to lie empty and drained on her bed. She did not sleep.

More details tiptoed in as she relived the hazy madness of the most recent past. She had, she recalled, the evening before last, dressed carefully in clean clothes on a clean body. She had postured smart and sexy before the small mirror, standing on a chair to check the image of her legs.

She had packed a handbag with cigarettes and money, comb and handkerchief, no valuables, no personal details. She walked happy and determined cool along the streets. Her first drink was a beer as she surveyed the scene in the crowded bar and checked her stomach for an absence of butterflies that would mean release, that she could go home without getting what she wanted. Her stomach, or more accurately, her cunt, fluttered and seemed quite confident, light-hearted and amused. She shifted on the stool and gazed, empty-eyed but seeing, at the crowd.

Her first and only criterion was physical attraction. She had located three possibilities by the end of the second beer. Two of these had located her and, being friends, they were commenting to each other on her intent, her possibilities. Mary didn't wait for their decision, but joined their table saying in low English, 'Would you boys like to buy me a drink?' They didn't understand the words, only the effect, so Mary felt confident that she could script her role in Hollywood fast talk and not appear absurd to anyone but herself. And she intended to be amused. She smiled, conspirator, and drank whisky and laughed and laughed.

Her bald laughter reassured the men that she would come across, was playing their game, so they took her to other bars where there was music and dancing and then to the fourth floor of a warehouse, a party where the recorded music was rock'n'roll and Mary danced some more and drank some more and allowed herself to be led off to someone's bed where one of the men took off her skirt and his own trousers and kissed her generously and drunkenly and nicely enough until she pushed him down and closed her eyes and clung to his heaving fucking. It was pleasant and somewhat relieving, sobering. Mary felt quite pleased with the ease of it all and went back to the party and danced some more, the night wore on, she could drink in earnest.

The dissipated life, Mary mused, as she wafted rather clumsily in time to the slow songs, watching, just for entertainment, the earnest talk of the party people. They shared a language she could pretend was not hers, and so, unlike her, they could not ignore the more formal manners of sexual life.

Late in the afternoon Mary Stevens abandoned her bed, her stillness and her hangover, dressed and walked again, this time without the smile. Today she walked the streets with a rawness, a subdued and deeper rawness of intent. Today the drink would suffice. But she went, caught in the déjà vu simplicity of yesterday, to the same street, the same bar. She looked for the same stool but it was occupied by another woman. Mary waited, standing at the counter, until another stool became vacant. She perched, discomforted by its other-bum warmness. She sat chain-smoking, sipping whisky, staring straight ahead. Slowly the whisky did its stuff, shoulders slumped, relaxed. She lifted a hand from the glass and rubbed her neck, bending the left shoulder up and dropping it. The whisky warmed her and dulled the noises of the bar into a comfortable soundtrack.

Jim, from the night before, appeared beside her, smiling but a little wary, reluctant. Mary turned her head, smiled, nodded, turned away. She bought him a whisky and he relaxed into her obvious casualness. Tonight they were reduced to the same level, the known and unknown, familiar and strange. Like, Mary thought, two spurned lovers at the others' wedding. They knew each other's desperation.

Their shared despair neutralised morality and judgment, dissolved all meanings in a foaming bowl of honesty (or pragmatism). They picked each other up again, drinking, steadily and quietly until the threat of boredom (intoxication) saw them off to another bar, more music, some dancing.

This bar was different from all the others. There was sawdust on the floor and a glamorous air of beyond-despair camaraderie, the shared drunkenness of the crowd. Mary felt repelled and delighted and accepted by the guzzled toothless leers, the generous gestures of the women, the optimistic threats of the young men whose thinness and youth were soon to be accentuated by the ageing that drink would insinuate into their pale skin, their greying hair slicked down with natural oiliness, the sweaty sleeping-off of the grog of yesterday.

Mary and Jim drank on, watching the antics of the older women who accepted alcohol and danced parodies of parodies of sexuality and fun. The band played cha-chas and American pop songs as Mary and Jim staggered (they imagined they strolled leisurely) out on to the street and the few houses' distance to where Jim just happened to live. Mary and Jim took all their clothes off as a sign of their intimacy, as assistance to their saturated erotic needs. They lay and rolled and stroked and kissed and smelled and groaned and sighed and writhed and drunken-slow and drunken-gentle, then sobering-rough and sober-urgent for it to be over, for the space to pass out to exist — they fucked. The climax of the expected, the known, the ordinary, the sordid.

Mary Stevens lay on her back smoking and drinking the dregs of the whisky, waiting for this man to get off, go to sleep. She scuttled from the bed and out into the streets. The sun had risen hours ago. She had missed the romance of dawn.

But no. That is not what happened. Mary fled the place as soon as Jim began to snore. She caught a taxi home in the darkness and fell fully clothed into bed, still drunk. She awoke an hour later, still dark, she lay rigid and determined. I will not wake up. It's too early. I will not wake up and face (all) the awful memories, the years of regret and recrimination stretching empty before me. No. Yes. I will catch the early train to the coast and be in England for breakfast. And so she did.

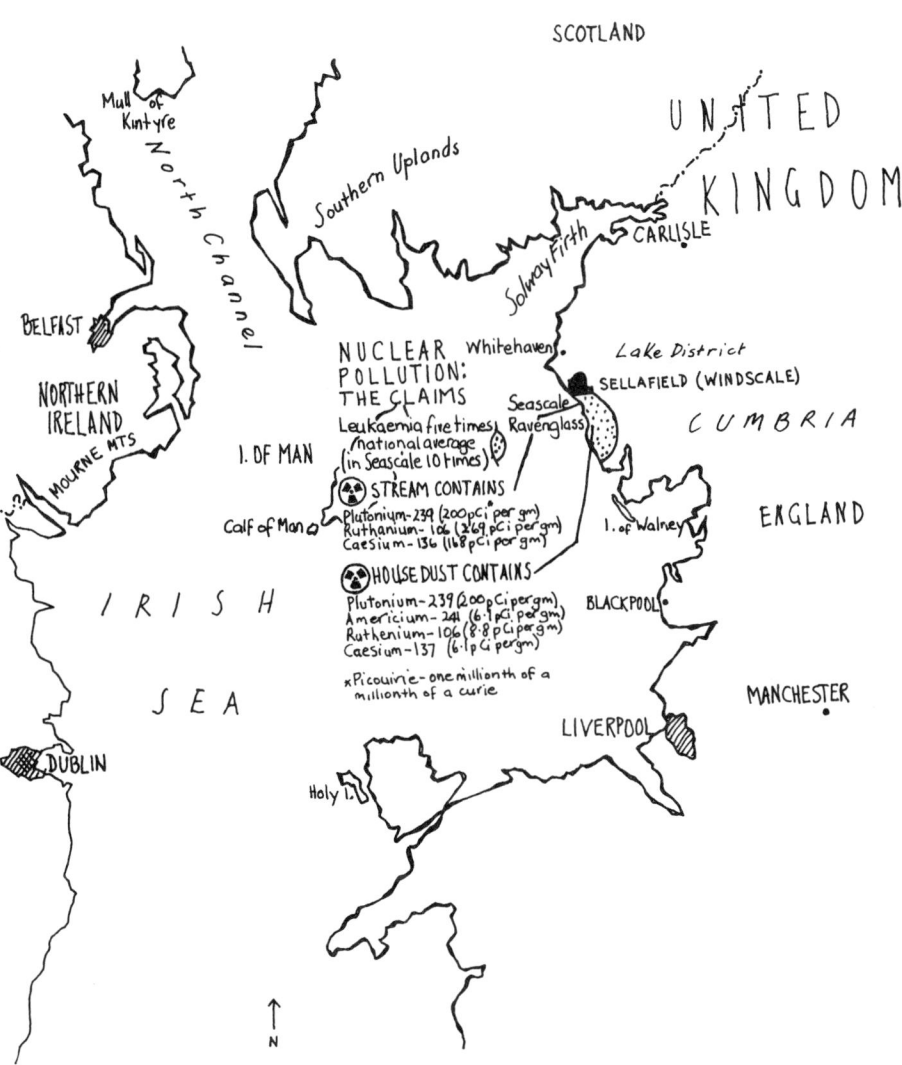

22

Mary Stevens in London

The moon was in Sagittarius as she crossed the channel. Luck. Venus low to the horizon. Mars nowhere to be seen. She gazed at the stars and conjured Edith's London address from the chaotic filing system of her brain: 12A Tulip Street, Kensington. (From such details are fictions made.) The phone number was gone forever, off in a brain cell zapped by fear or alcohol or just the years passing. She walked from the tube station, knocked on the door and fainted on to the hall floor.

Edith and Cecil had been in London a month or so. Cecil was settling in. At first the stiffness froze him out and he laughed too loud and told too many stories (his accent broadening) of the distance and space, the beaches and skies, Australia the landscape; it sounded like another planet in these close London evenings.

Then, as if he had pressed the correct switch, struck the right tone, dropped the right name, Cecil began to be a success. He was in dinner-party demand, asked to read at Bingham's and the Society, interviewed and quoted, he became quite full of himself, and Edith, bored and slightly miffed, ceased to accompany him.

Thus Mary Stevens, dressed like a dishrag, her hair like a birch broom in a fit, was a gift to Edith who could now entertain and dress, cart about and chat on to. Yes. Edith was pleased her old and unfamiliar friend had turned up. If only she would go outside the house. Mary Stevens resisted unsuccessfully and it was on her fourth day that Dagmar caught up with her in the park. They sat on a bench, 'This is. . . impossible. . . unbearable.' Mary smiled at Dagmar. They were friends despite the tension, the exercise of power. In ordinary life they would have enjoyed each other's company and kept a smooth distance. 'Give me a reason,' Mary demanded quietly. 'It's your job. You can do it. And the end justifies the means. It's a way of buying you life for a while. Is this too extreme?'

The sky clouded over. A wind came up and the park emptied. The two women sitting on the bench looked like obstinate lovers engaged in a serious trauma. They walked arm in arm along the path.

Mary Stevens returned to the Kensington flat, packed her belongings, picked up Cecil's car keys from the hall table, stole his car and drove north out of London, and west.

Eventually the green of the country, the matters of maps and petrol, money and feeling hungry, cups of tea when you get to the sea, an ocean grey and subdued by comparison, changed the notion of this being a moment out of time to the ordinary sort of journey on which decisions are made.

The anonymity of a tourist, the great disguise of something ordinary. Mary Stevens sat in a hotel lounge room. The future unfaced rolls on anyway. These escapes. These escapades. This extremism. It has to stop.

For Mary Stevens confusion and disorder prevail. She carefully 'considers the beginning'. (*I Ching*)

She felt by now that she made decisions on the basis of fantasy, or on how the words, arranged in a particular order, made a difference. To see so simply is to reduce the danger, the fear, to make choices possible. It began to seem possible. Out of all the conflict, out of the prevailing confusion and disorder of Paris, and not just hers, she could retreat, fall back, escape from and consider (in the space created) where to escape to.

An Italian coffee shop. In London, yes. In rural England no such lovely thing. She longed for Australia then. She filled thermoses in the boarding-house kitchen and walked through the wind to a place of shelter between rocks looking over the Irish Sea. The locals said the sea was closed. Contaminated, the newspapers would eventually announce (as if it had only just happened, right in time for the deadline) by plutonium waste, that, in the way of these nuclear things, hadn't behaved as predicted, hadn't sunk safely to the sea-bed. Unseasonal weather (which is the way of weather too) had brought it back, beach and rock awash with a dull gleam turning to dust as dehydration occurred beneath an unseasonal sun. Summer 1982. England. Northern hemisphere. Mary Stevens considered (her) fate. Or resistance.

Palmistry, tea leaves, I Ching, astrology, guilt, fantasy, there had to be a clear way out of these years. She knew there was not, could not be. Small movements, ordinary things, life was more like that and she couldn't break the rules alone. She wasn't alone. There was power — an organisation albeit secreted and discrete — that pushed her around, that cleared jungle and picked up cheques, that made big steps easy by breaking big rules. She could use. . . could she?. . . she could use that. . . would she?. . . could she without becoming trapped?. . . again. . . she carefully considered the beginning. . .

How had she put herself in the way of this life which she had come, she admitted now, to like, to accept as all right, right, her life? She believed that she had not made decisions then, or had not chosen what had come from. Now she would make decisions and presume that other, quite other things would occur. She had learned something about power. This — that it does not reside in the individual.

She walked the headlands away from the nuclear reactor, this was to place yourself in danger. The unseen. Which breath carried poison? Which rock sat on was the one? Which rock pool washed her feet with more than sodium chloride?

(Powerlessness before the large, the unspeakable, the unbelieveable. And hadn't England always found its subjects dispensable. Mary Stevens' country had been white-settled for just that easy reason, the debris of the industrial revolution shipped off to that most un-British place, Australia. And wouldn't Margaret Thatcher love to have such a clear solution to her unemployed millions who have turned, just as necessarily but with a good deal more organisation, to crime to survive.)

She came to flat country swarming with ghosts and spirits and crossword puzzle roads you get the hang of after two days. Grey afternoons that clear at night. Watch the sky. Watch the lights of aeroplanes off over the horizon, blink, white. Red. Satellites spied and surprising, reminding. They had asked her what she was prepared to do now that she had refused to do what they asked and given a choice she knew immediately. Pine Gap. The crucial US transmission and reception base in Australia. Pine Gap, thank you. Get me a job at Pine Gap. Leave me alone.

It could be done. Yes.

They preened and smiled. Rock and Stone, if you can imagine such intransigence vain. Their protégé had learned well.

Mary Stevens' decision involved a great deal of compromise. She would have to go to the United States, spend a year there becoming someone else to be trained and taught the intricacies of receiving and deciphering messages from satellites, transferring them 'home' — this was the easy part. Harder was the persona. To be, in these most paranoid of times, a facsimile of an American in that country, to become Sally Forster from Dallas U, a laughing girl with conventional views and belief in the American way. Our heroine is unbelieveable.

To become Sally Forster, American agent, cloistered in the centre of Australia unable to own her own country, unable to, for instance, gaze wistfully at the desert and adore — her cover required a rather troubled disdain, this land, the Yanks would decry, what other use for it but this, a barren empty place as if it was meant for just this, us, the US supreme intelligence connection, here at the centre is the centre, that which keeps the balance for us.

The real Sally Forster, the one from Dallas U, one of a million alike with good teeth and no parental money or influence, no close relatives, accepted the offer of a suitable wardrobe, a Corvette with NY number-plates, another name, a place in Harvard, in a few years Wall Street and no memory of the past. She accepted and Mary Stevens was in, a bit of work on the mid-west accent, drilling a life history that she memorised easily, so much like what she'd seen at the movies. She was whisked around the country for views of first home, hospital where born, church her parents married in, high school and the details, drug stores and lover's lanes, year books and classmates' names; she took it in and dreamed the emotions not so removed from her Australian own. The American history was harder, the detail, they were imbued from birth with an idiosyncratic version and she had to cram it in from books and old newspapers but the key meanings were lost, she had no reference point, no emotional place to hang such obsessive love of country, such unquestioning belief in destiny. She faked it. For it seemed like to much fakery to her, and she turned her mind to computers, a world complete, a history recent and rich, a language free of ideology and emotion, she studied and learned and was pushed and coached to become a National Security Agent, Class 3, top secrecy cleared, the heart of the beast.

1983 Nov 11. Women's protest camp. Women for Survival. Close Pine Gap.
In 1983 some other women would pick the heart of the matter. They would, in veiled hats and baggy shorts and wind-swept faces construct a powerful symbolic by their presence and resistance, their brave but powerless actions against the might and strength of the USA. To place yourself in such a way at such a time, to construct the image that makes the reality, that makes message and statement, is an act that exists unchangeably and changes forever the conventions of politics and diplomacy and security. (Does it?)

Mary Stevens could not own this either, once inside, secreted, working for not against, she occupied a duplicitous position, the ambiguous, probably the inevitably conventional position of the opposition that, by its existence, continues to construct the status quo.

For example, by being a spy, any spy for any cause, you justify all spies. All measures against. By constructing the supra-secret you validate every ordinary security measure, every transgression of individual rights. It is an argument not dissimilar to that applied to bureaucrats; if you are one you support the system, if you wish to subvert, to challenge or change, your effect is always less than the support you give to the system by working for it. If you worked effectively against it you would simply be sacked.

Mary Stevens had, in her reflections on decisions, picked it right. She had put herself in the way of the crucial, the elemental flow of truth. She had access and skill, she could filter through to the others some pieces of information that would inform for subversion, but only so long as she remained beyond suspicion. And she could not, when the crises came, prevent, for example, the shooting down of the KAL 007 or the launching of the first missiles into the Middle East.

Perhaps she could blow the lot (and herself) up, would that be the way to go, anonymous and effective, a decision made alone, a single anarchistic act that would, she knew with certainty, be transformed from intention to a superpower contingency — perhaps the women on the gate would be blamed, or some crank from a country more strategic than Grenada, Turkey perhaps, and Dagmar would spit and stalk and damn her in hell for rampant individualism and the luxury of martyrdom. They walk away from consequences.

Dense clouds. No rain from the western regions

The rain comes. There is rest. Stay.
August-September 1982.
The elements (climate in stagnation). Seven years of drought. The weather has become tepid, the long process into drought, the absence of all suddenness — then dry thunder. The drought is slow, on the land so many things can't be done, no crops no water, the cattle are driven along the roadsides, the long paddock. The clouds are like a mirage on the horizon. The thunder is like the sound of guns.

In the city street the boy-men wear clothes across which is written 'cannon fodder' and you can watch the rain out over the sea. The Americans approach warfare with thousands of weapons and tens of thousands of men. They squander both. That is wealth and democracy. The squandering of men.

23

Susan was forty-three

Susan Miller was forty-three in 1983. She worked as office manager and de facto director in Joan Stevens' persistent absence, Joan's dedicated spinster schoolteacher act was disguise and desire. Susan hardly ever saw her, hadn't talked to her often enough on the phone to recognise her voice. Joan Stevens certainly couldn't be accused of meddling in the business. She kept a vague distance, insisting only on certain hours of computer time (all her data was automatically encrypted by the key pad at her home terminal), and reviewing the monthly audits which were sent to her routinely on the 28th of each month (or the next Monday) and were returned by her by the fifth of the next. Susan paid routine attention to the postmark of the return mail and learned, as if by accident over the years, that Sydney, the Riverina and the South Coast of NSW were Joan Stevens' regular tracks with several false trails, once to Canberra (she was just passing through), twice to the Sunshine Coast (Noosa) and once to Adelaide. (But that was at Festival time and perhaps she was in a cultural phase. Certainly she brought back some nice South Australian wine.) Susan was offered an excellent dry red when she broke the forms and dropped the December audit at Miss Stevens' solid old house in 'Footscray Heights'. Susan was curious.

The house was in an ambiguous state. Half-packed suitcases of holiday gear stood on the lounge room floor, the dining room was neat and decorated, hands had spent time arranging fresh flowers, a tray of spirits and apéritifs on the sideboard, the kitchen fridge was well-stocked but boxes of groceries side by side on the kitchen table signalled something, departure?

Susan was surprised to see Joan walk into the office on the following Monday. Joan smiled and said hello, asked her if Stone was about and could Susan bring them both in some coffee made from the bag of fresh grounds she produced from her basket. Susan obliged like any good servant and helped herself to the dregs. She spent a quiet day at her desk, aching to minister to the needs of her superiors in order to eavesdrop on this unusual and therefore serious flurry of management at work. Susan was kept back late that day to send off a series of extremely confidential telexes. She put them through by nine and left. Joan and Stone settled in for a long wait for the replies.

Amelia, waking to a fine New York day perused their words over her endless black coffee breakfast. By midday she and Dagmar had agreed on the reply. Joan received them alone at 6.30 a.m., she took both copies in her basket and drove through the sunrise to the river country. Grace made her a cup of tea and they spread out over the kitchen table deciphering, recoding, plugging away at the mass of material. It took them four days before Joan caught up on her sleep sufficiently to make the long drive back. She met Amelia at Tullamarine and they talked nineteen to the dozen as they drove through the peak-hour traffic to the house in Footscray. Susan came across them installed in the office at 8.30 a.m., as if they owned the place, she commented to Rose the typist. 'Well, don't they?' she replied.

'I wouldn't be too sure of that anymore, there's been some peculiar late nights around here.'

'You don't think we've been hit by the recession do you, I mean, the newspapers say. . .'

24

Joan was in a flat spin

Joan was in a flat spin. Had been so for weeks. Things weren't going as planned. She called Grace and Sarah in, and invited Susan for the first time to a formal meeting of the hens. What to do about this delay in Paris.

Joan had always had a feeling about this Parsley person. And then, late in the night the bells rang on the telex machine. Stalemate. More time. Might have to give up on this pawn. Supposed to be in America by now. Settled into Wall Street, neatly placed to effect the redistribution of the world's wealth.

Even Amelia, who was only truly happy in New York and who was not supposed to know Joan anymore, even Amelia had flown into Tullamarine in the middle of winter. The five women, the hen's party reassembled, sprawled on the lounge room floor before an open fire.

They talked a rambling conversation, from funny to serious to gossip to speculation to wild guesses:
'If you want something done, do it yourself.'
'My daughter. My daughter. How could Irving and Dagmar be so stupid?'
'Or so smart.'
'She *is* your daughter.'
'That might make her tailor-made.'
'And vulnerable. And me responsible.'
'We are all responsible.'
'What about Maude and the rest in Moscow. Good odds we'll never see them again. And Frances in Israel and Jo in Beirut and Annette in South Africa and and and. . .'

There was a knock on the door. Freeze. Make tea. Knit furiously. Dagmar. Jet-lagged around the eyes but perfectly groomed as always. 'There's been a development that is not entirely against our interests.'

Pine Gap remained a useful installation despite the apparent KGB infiltration. Out there in the clear desert air, a compound, closed off, focused, exclusive and polished smooth; as close as men become to machines. They work crisp shifts and drink cool beer in air-conditioned rooms. The receivers purr and click, esoteric secrets kept safe in most sophisticated codes, they zap and climb, combine and travel the ozone layer with ease, the very essence of an eloquent silence.

The desert stretched away from this in all directions. The red dirt. The roads bitumenised to full stops. No sidetracks or turn-offs. The sun very bright each day. The domes of the complex loom from the earth. The clouds are purple and white high up near the birds that hover like B-52s for the kill, specks in the blue.

It was never quite quiet. Cars came and went. Muzak played. Sprinklers whirred on green lawn patches and children shrieked at play and zoomed and bang-banged in this safest of places. There were even a few pedestrians, though each of the buildings is connected to each of the others by underground tunnels — of course. But there are a few men and women walking or jogging, to and fro. The buildings and bubbles were numbered after colours: 6 Red, 14 Black, 39 Green. There were no pinks or purples, no yellow, those colours were kept outside the fences, all around, stretching into the huge distances, away away, the country seemed to race, a thousand miles to the sea. No army could march that far. No missile stay true and invisible. They hoped.

Pine Gap is peopled by those adapted to airconditioning. White skin, fair hair, blue eyes, even teeth, strong jaw. Ordinary. Perfect. These workers were as close as the laywomen of the resistance could get to locating the powerful (if only on the symbolic level, if knowledge is power and access to buttons (key boards) the real danger). The money might change hands in illusions called banks but so too the hands might change and from Zurich to Florida to Guam to Hong Kong to Sydney to New York, bringing it all back home. Geography might describe and governments be reinitialled, weapons renamed, banks might become caches become drug runners or another (ground) war-zone. And still it looks the same.

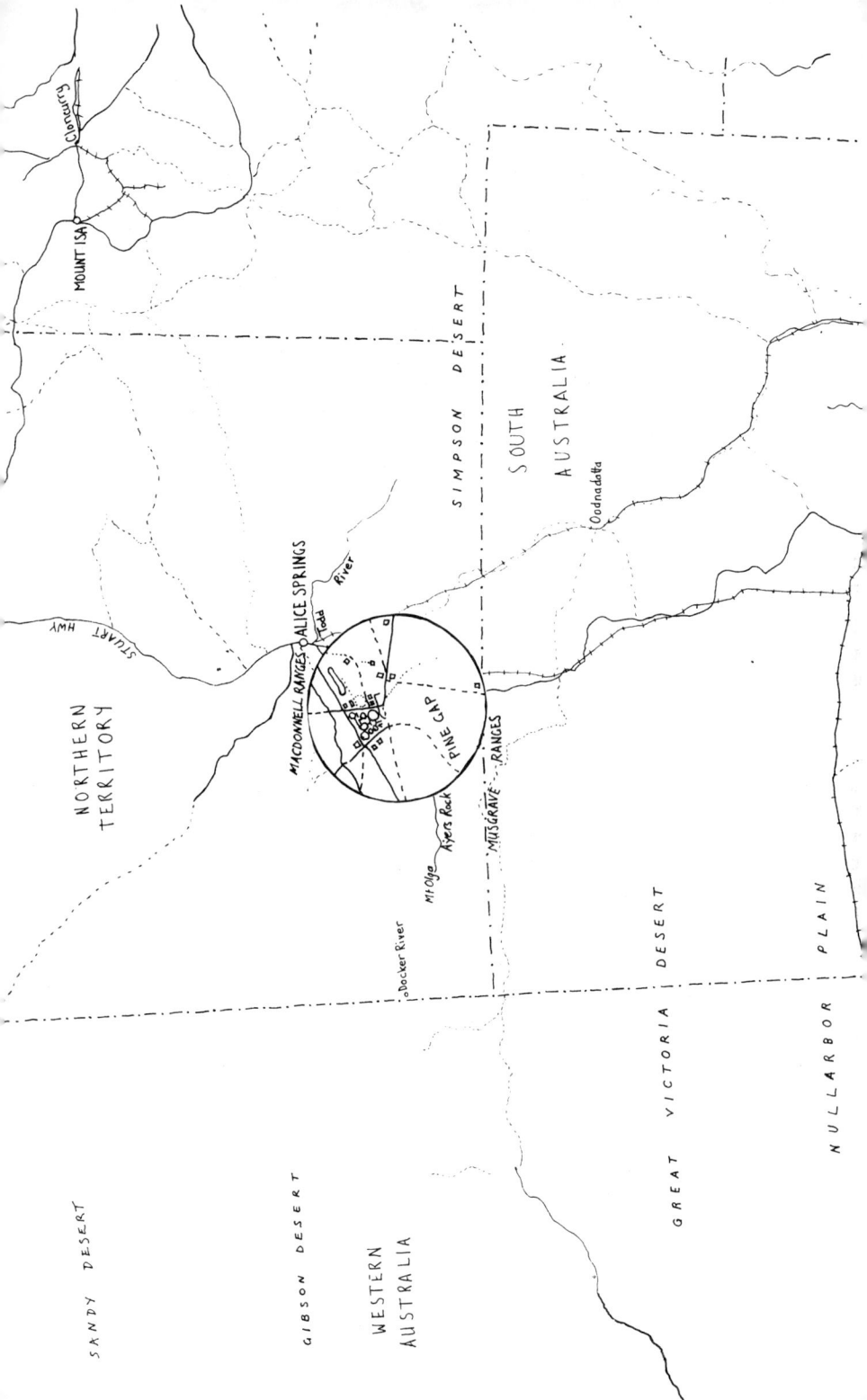

'Look,' said Amelia, angry at their confusion, 'it doesn't matter. Whatever happens looks like endless repeats of B-grade movies anyway. She's said she'll go to Pine Gap and we can organise that. It might, just might, be useful. Remember, random factors. Lives still get lived and people can still think and we've had some success with the stock exchange idea and we know a lot more now that actions have been taken. We have disturbed the status quo. They still don't know who killed Crane or why Cecil Evans really had to go to London; the Russians don't know that Andropov's wife is smart enough to hide our friend Maude on her kitchen staff. The ripples are relentless once set in motion. Cheer up Joan. It's not so bad. At least your daughter will be coming home.'

25

Black flag in a landscape

Black flag in a landscape.
It is night. Moonlight.
The landscape is flat.
A pool of muddy water reflects a mirror image of the moon and stars. The water up close is muddy. Tyre tracks. Cattle tracks. The carcass of a stuck cow.

The black flag in the flat country is a mirage Grace sees every morning. She gets up before dawn, when it is still dark, then deepest blue, to do the housework, grading the back paddock in preparation for the crop they cannot plant because of the rain. Its absence.

She rests in the high heat of the afternoon. She is asleep again at nine.

Grace did not anticipate problems, sit waiting for the sky to fall. Stanley had taken the mob to the long paddock and she stayed on the property, keeping the horses alive with hand-feeding.

In 1982 Grace took a job in town. Even rich graziers are affected in a drought, in its sixth year now. In Sydney Grace had free accommodation at The Women's Club in exchange for a little supervisory nonsense (housekeeper and nightwatcher) and a bit of cash. This way she managed to keep the sharefarmer and his wife on to see to the horses. This way she managed to be the mistress of that rare and prized place, a 'safe house'.

The club was a graceful building, marble foyer, rickety lift, walls hung with paintings, Grace Cossington Smith and Margaret Preston among many others; there was chintz in the sitting room and a piano, grand. It was barely used by the country women who made up its ageing membership, a safe house apart from the weekly forays made into it by a bevy of businesswomen (aspiring Merchant Bankers, Tax Accountants, Stock Brokers and Management Consultants, Record Company Executives and clever heiresses), Grace was at liberty to study for future uses.

Grace played the horses and the stock exchange, tiding the property and herself over, feeding a few birds off the one scam. Sometimes she could be seen, full length fur coat and very good pearls, off to the Opera House and later, the fur coat over silk pyjamas, she monitored the 'bugs' in the Tattersalls Club a few doors down.

Not Quite Delores Del Rio

(The sort of thing Edith was saying in 1981.)
Hiding. In hiding. Inside. On the inside. Who is hiding who and who. . . Night owls. Heavy curtains lined and drawn against the cold in London and against other things. Edith couldn't see why or what, but most definitely things were not quite right, not quite right at all. Her friend Mary convalesces quickly (from an unnamed condition) goes out, comes back, steals Cecil's car and disappears. Two days later a strange woman arrives at the door and introduces herself as Sarah, a friend of Mary's.

I asked her in for a cup of tea. She is Australian. Well enough dressed to make me comfortable. She wanted particularly to see Mary, I told her the story and then we talked on about Cecil. She knows his work she said, and then prevailed upon me to invite her to stay, which I did. Cecil came home and we all had dinner together and then went up to bed because we had all had a tiring day. Sarah went straight out after breakfast, we arranged to meet for afternoon tea. I went to the address she had given me, pushed open the double doors and walked across a stark courtyard. Another woman came out to meet me and we went into a large room off the courtyard with tables and white cloths and bentwood chairs and teapots and urns and two or three sorts of cake and a general air of informal cafeteria about it.

(Workers' tea break here. A private-public place, a couple of women put the tea and cake together and do the dishes through the day, refill milk jugs, wipe down tables, put salt and pepper out at lunchtime, two cakes before ten and two more by one, sandwiches usually did for the lunch time though Alice stayed back and did the fruit cakes, they were a good standby.)

The time it takes to have a cup of tea and a piece of cake (and maybe a second cup and a cigarette but that's the limit) was the crucial length of time required to display the choreography of assignation, question, answer, decision. Action.

Sarah and Dagmar and I shared a large pot of Earl Grey and other things in the tea room under the public building. Later Sarah and I went to a car rental place, the hairdressers, two department stores that deliver and a rather particular sort of travel agent. I got my passport out of the bank and told Cecil I was going to Switzerland and then Rome with Sarah who was a friend of Mary's and he said fine fine let me know when you're due to return and I'll meet the plane, perhaps I could fly out to Rome and we could take a boat back like in the thirties novels you like reading so much. He laughed. Cecil knew what was up. 'Edith's travelling in Europe with a friend.' He liked the tone of that. It could have been risqué or innocent.

Tony Naismith, Sarah and Edith skied down the Matterhorn and watched a chap fall before them. They helped him up and behind the layers and goggles a familiarity, a seventies memory, and they went on their way.
Sheer coincidence.
Sarah and Edith disappear.
They might have been killed for their knowledge, or gone in pursuit.
Young Edith is certainly capable of adventuring.

Gloria Stanley arrived in London to find Cecil alone one night at the Kensington flat. She explains. Mary Stevens was their target, she escaped from under his nose.
'But I didn't know. And I can't believe...'
'It doesn't matter. We'll catch up with her.'
'Though she did steal my car. That was suspicious. I got it back...'
'Where's Edith?'
'Gone. Left me. For another woman. What am I to do?'
'Go back to Melbourne, dear Cecil, and think not another thing about it.'
'Will I get a second chance? Will you contact me again if there's anything I can do, though I rather liked Mary Stevens, in a

downwardly mobile sort of way. Old friend of Edith's you know.'
'Yes. We know all about it. Now. It's too late. They've got some remarkable sort of security these amateurs, these female adventurers.'

The whole story threatened to come out in 1985 and what a sorry tale. By then the damage had been done and Cecil, knowing so little and knowing so much, was dispensed with, an umbrella dart as he walked to his lunch at the Melbourne Club. He didn't recognise Bob Baxter walking toward him, he was absorbed in the last couplet of a love-lost sonnet, to the memory of Edith. He had never seen her again.

Cecil's scandalous death was a smokescreen (and a scare tactic), so no more accurate questions would be asked about how Australia was no longer a place safe for American bases or about the Funny Business of international currency and drugs.

Ah. Such a happy ending. I think not. They made it an anti-Russian scare which allowed the state to invoke harsher (looser) laws on matters of evidence. Conspiracy is breath.

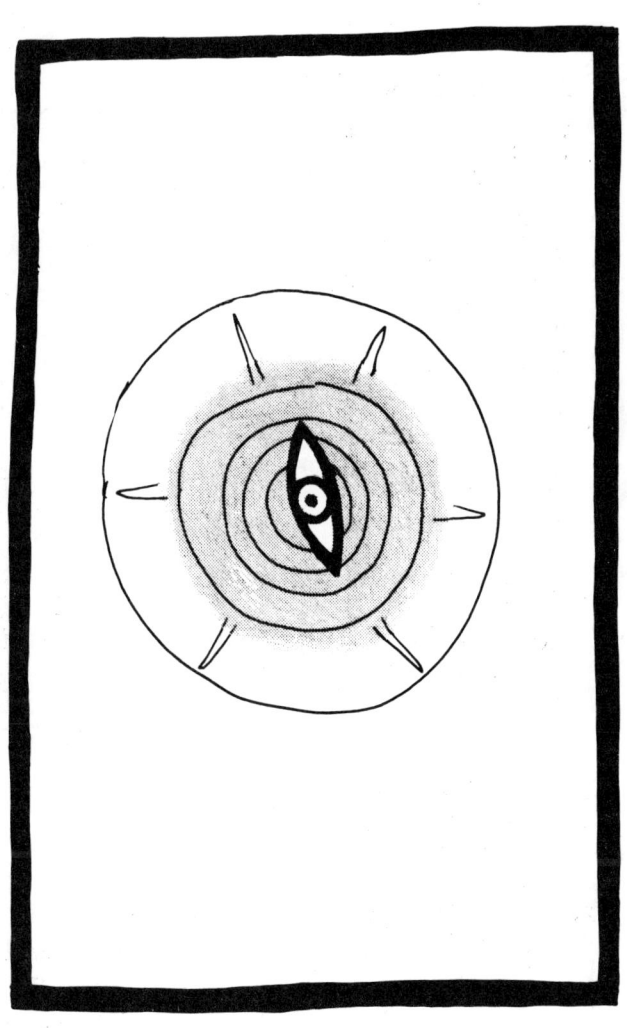

Honolulu. 4.2.83.

Dear Mother,

By the time you get this I will be back. I flew in around the 7th and will go to the house at Grenella for a week or so. I have much to tell you but don't think I can make it to Melbourne. I hope you can make it to the coast before I have to leave again, sometime around the end of March. I have heard that the country is very dry. Four years of drought & misery be terrible. The bushfires were front page in LA before I left. I guess Sam and Sue's place was wiped out as others, but, that is so sad, they worked hard for that. Please give them my love. Hope to see you soon.

Lor. Mary.

Mrs Joan Attius
41 Moore Street
Footscray Heights,
Victoria.
Australia.

26

The end of something

Guerella, March 1983. (The End of the Drought.)

Mary Stevens arrives at her mother's holiday house in a lime green hired car. The bush is soft colours and sunshine. The air is still. The sea calm. She arrives, eats, goes straight to sleep.

In the night she wakes to hear the rain on the tin roof. It drums. The wind blusters up to a gale. The sea builds and crashes. It rains all the next day, the night, another day and another night. Mary Stevens walks in the rain, along the beaches by wild seas, unimaginable power, smashing over rocks that have been dry for years. Visual spectacle. She watches and watches, going up old tracks barely marked to the top of the cliffs. Close to the edge she watches whole trees buffeted in the surf and placed, like consciousness, on the gleaming rock platforms. They are sculptures.

She takes off all her clothes and soaps up in the overflow from the tank. There is no one else around. She hears the crack of a tree split by the gale, watches the top branch fall, checks the power lines and tanks and finds wet wood to saw up and drag under the verandah. She makes a fire inside to dry off her clothes and runners and sleeps in front of it at night.

On Tuesday morning the sky is blue before dawn. She wakes and watches through the window, it turns grey, is streaked with orange, the streaks are promising. The rain stops. She gets up and walks again. All the beaches have changed. The sea subsides a bit. She collects driftwood into piles as she goes and watches the sky for the first birds to emerge from their mysterious shelters.

The wind turns cold, whips the bush, a cool sunshine. Inside the shack Mary searches for the letters she posted to herself so long ago. It is time to recall. She doesn't find them so drives to Malua Bay to check the Post Office. They aren't there either. The woman in the Post Office is new and doesn't remember any such letters, 'But we get so many, I mean I don't pry, but oh, what did you say your name was, yes, Mary Stevens, been here for a few weeks, didn't come through the mail, handed in to my son, he does the counter on weekends. Here you are.'

Dear Mary,
    Imagine if your mother had opened them. My dear, you must be more careful. We cannot guarantee your safety now. Please. Recognise the danger in the game. We cannot have you knowing that which might be useful under interrogation. Some memories serve no purpose and are merely dangerous.

                                                        Love
                                                        Dagmar

Mary Stevens drives through the sunshine, the bush steaming after ten inches of rain, the drought is breaking. She saws the driftwood into armfuls, working up a sweat on the beach. A jet flies low off the coast, under radar, so fast as it flashed between the headlands. It could have been a mirage.

That night she wakes. Sleepless. Turns on the radio.
It's a saxophone-before-dawn time.
It is blue music on a black night. No moon. No stars.
It's the moment before a story begins. A moment just that and no more.
There is no silence.
Spiders talk in whispers.
The moment of illumination. Dawn. A saxophone plays.
Mary Stevens appears. She is a middle-sized woman, quite plain in the grey light. She re-reads a letter, folds it, puts it away in a book at random, just one that is close at hand.
No.

I would have liked the final paragraph of the novel to read:
I suppose history will say Mary Stevens finally became partisan in Beirut. For commitment must be the emotional response to such witnessing. But the partisans and the committed do not make the difference. The witnesses witness also their own powerlessness.
At least Mary Stevens carried a gun.
but the plot twisted away from such profundity.
You get this piece of polemic instead.

In this novel there is no depression, no unemployment, nobody gets retrenched, there are no elections, no coups, no wars. There is no attempt to represent 'reality'. It does not intervene. And yet there is some purpose, some sense to a scenario that is put, like a suitcase on an interstate train, to leave and arrive (by fiction) mysteriously changed.

There is some point to fiction. To the made. We live in a world of no truth.

The USA and USSR are essential to each other's existence.

States.
The State.
It is, in anyone's book a statement of fact.
We all allow the State its existence.
Some to rail against.
Others to fall back, vote. The simple silence.
Others to profit.
And reformist positions are soaked in champagne and novelists know they cannot change a thing and rock bands get rich and Australian blacks live in an invaded country, just, and women, their historic absence, their unremitting presence, remain ambiguous. And all the way along people live their little lives, each. The State cannot prevent that.

Damned random factors.
And history requires adventurers and martyrs and those lucky enough to have the time.

The author has had time to consider her prose, her scenario.
She is self-conscious.
It is not complete.
There is no end.
The characters might speak but in the end there is no end and only she speaks.
To have read this far you have been made
like a work of fiction
a detective
an historian.
There are gaps in every record.
They can be filled.

Mary Stevens had gone, she had left the beach at Guerella and her illuminating letter fast, off across country in the high heat of summer, she left the car in Adelaide and flew to Alice Springs. This was an agreed-upon route. The Americans could have watched her all the way, apart from the three nights at the beach when they would have had to be lucky to catch her and to make the connection with Joan Stevens. She was clean. Queer though that she choose to spend her stay in beautiful Sydney in a boarding house in Redfern.

(And Miss Tree could have told the Americans everything they wanted to know and so much more than they wanted to hear. They merely watched. Miss Tree would have been insistent. She and her girls would never have anything to hide. Nothing but a reputable establishment thank you. You're not from the council are you, they want to put a hotel or a park here you know. Taking good homes from people who have lived there without any trouble all their lives. I was born in this house. It was built by my father after the war, the first. He died the day we moved in. Never slept a night here. So my mother took in boarders. Young ladies. Some grew old here. We've got mostly young women here again, and it's harder for them what with no jobs. We try to keep things nice but we're too old to have anything permanent to offer them. They try and move on when they get on their feet. I guess we tell too many stories about the old days. Mother and me. She's still alive you know. And active. Hasn't had a day sick in her life. But it's hard for the young ones. To listen. Mary always listens when she comes here. She used to come in at night and I'd make her a cup of tea and she'd say, OK Anna, talk to me. Tell me a story. I need to hear something real. And I'd tell her about the war and she'd do the peas for dinner and then she'd tell me about some incident at the office and Mother would laugh at her sharp little descriptions and I would scold her for being so harsh. She would stare at the pictures on the wall and talk about being somewhere else one day. And she went. Never sent us a postcard or anything but sometimes letters came for her or were returned here when someone she had written to had moved. Perhaps she'll come back here to live now she's been away so long. These days it's not a matter of whether you like someone, it's the familiar that matters. I'm too old for new people. And I'm glad young Susan's back for a while, though she's another one who never writes. It's a pity really, how else can we remember.

The Americans might have said, had they taken time to listen, 'Precisely, the less put on paper these days the better', but even they, in their total recall world of the serious, failed to notice that the very Susan Miller they might have been interested in knowing had slipped passed their ears as idle gossip.)

Instead Mary Stevens arrived at Alice Springs and disappeared. Has not been heard of since. Susan Miller left Melbourne for New York with Dagmar. New skills to learn. Grace returned to The Women's Club where she lived as housekeeper and on-site manager through the renovations to the building and until the drought broke when she returned to the farm. Sarah escaped to London and Edith and the brief romance of travelling freely. She would return to Melbourne and manage the company, for two years only she told Joan firmly, as if tone of voice could convince, 'You will have to leave teaching then Joan, and take over, I do not want to be tied to this.' Joan returned to the classroom and the nightwork and pined a lot for Amelia who had left for France threatening never to return. Of course, nothing went according to plan.